# WHO IS GOING TO HEAVEN?

## JIM CLAYTON

WINEPRESS WP PUBLISHING

ISBN 1-57921-252-2
Library of Congress Catalog Card Number: 99-66109

This book is dedicated to each of you who read its pages,
That its message
Will enrich your journey in life with our great God,
Or
Help you in your journey to truly know God
And to find your eternal, heavenly home with him.


And
to
April, Connor, and Eli

# ACKNOWLEDGMENTS

To Dr. Robert E. Webber, Ken DeRuiter, Marlene LeFever, Margaret Lachler, Sonja Cotterell, Robert and Janet Simpson, Mildred Clayton, Marie Marsh, my wife, Marcy, and many, many others who provided insight, advice, and encouragement in the creation of *Who Is Going to Heaven?* Many thanks to all of you.

Thanks to the late Bob Briner and his book, *Deadly Detours*, for helping confirm the philosophy contained in "The Churchman" story.

All persons in this book are fictional except the biblical characters and the following four people in "The Gang Banger" story:

- Steve Thompson, chaplain of the Good News Jail & Prison Ministry in the Cook County Jail.
- Bill Dillon, founder and director of Inner City Impact in the Humboldt Park area of Chicago.
- Gordon McLean, who works with gang members at the Juvenile Justice Ministry of Chicago Youth for Christ.
- Thomas Ray, former teacher at Von Humboldt Elementary School in Chicago.

# CONTENTS

# PROLOGUE

## SOMEWHERE IN TIME

*Long, long ago when time had just begun.*

Hey, wait just a minute! Was there ever a beginning to time? Did time just begin one fine day? Could time have started at some point far in the distant past?

Did God create time? Everything else was created by God. God tells us of his eternal existence. Could God have existed when there was no time frame, no space of time, no passing of time? Certainly. We cannot limit God. God is God. He created everything. Even time!

The bottom line is that time is very old, no matter when it was set in motion by God. And whether you believe the earth to be a few thousand or a few billion years of age, we are still but a dot in the spectrum of time.

Nevertheless, we are a very important dot to ourselves, which as a self-centered people is very natural. But we are also immensely important to God, since he himself created us and he places great value on us as a human race. We are, after all, a reflection of God, made in his own image.

Have you ever wondered what God did during all the time before we came on the scene? Ever wonder what he was God of? Certainly his own heaven. But, other worlds, other peoples? Are they still around? How would he relate to them? Were they, or are they, like us? Would they do wrong things like we do? Or would they be a perfect race of people? Probably not!

If not, how would God deal with their wrongdoing? Would God send his son to die for sin more than once? Once on Earth, again on that planet in galaxy Omega, five years later on another, and on and on it would go? If so, would that make Christ the sacrifice for the sin of the entire universe? Most of us would tend to think not, but who knows God's span of ideas and ways of doing things. Anything is possible with God.

God does what he wants to do. God rules. He has structured his world and universe with his plan. God deals with us the way he wants to. His plan is not one we can change or remake. God is the only one up there, the only game in town.

From the very beginning of human life, man has thought of his own death. He has speculated about his afterlife and what it will be like. As a result, throughout the history of man's spiritual journey, he has created many gods. There have been gods, to control his environment, influence his personal life, and determine his life after death.

Throughout man's history the concept of a god system has almost always been accepted by a large portion of people.

From cave dwellers to the Greeks and Romans, to our own American society, people have acknowledged a god creator in one form or another.

From the earliest times in human history, a common thread has woven through the fabric of man's spiritual pilgrimage: man is more than capable of creating a religious system that will meet his needs. Man has always been an expert in finding gods to fit neatly into his corner of the world.

There are certainly many mysteries we do not understand about our human existence. However, there is one indisputable fact: our universe, our world, the human race, you and I, were created in one way or another. We know we exist. We can see and hear and touch. We are real. At some place in time there had to be a beginning, somewhere, somehow!

Since that is true, we have a choice of two beliefs. The first is that our existence is just an occurrence that happened by accident, a fluke in the wind that somehow started somewhere in time with no intelligent force or power to influence its progress. This belief would mean our universe developed without design or control from an external source.

The second possible conclusion is that our universe did not occur by accident or random chance. Even though a sun may have exploded, eventually creating a planet we call Earth, that sun itself had to have a beginning. And if we were to go back further in time we would realize something had to be started first in order for all the rest to follow.

If one accepts the second belief, the obvious question would then be what created this first physical "thing" to come into our universe? Something cannot be started from within a vacuum. What power could have initiated this indescribable place in which we live. What would be the characteristics of a force this mighty and all encompassing? Certainly it would have required an intellect of immense proportions. Given the beauty of the earth and everything on the earth, this power had to possess a wide range of powerful emotions and imagination. The amount of energy needed would have been staggering. But even these descriptions are inadequate to describe the characteristics of the spectacular power that created our universe.

Man will probably never know how this extraordinary force did its creating, and the length of the creation process. But somewhere in time, as the world progressed through segments of unknown eons, this great power revealed itself to a creature called man, as he came on the timetable of earth's tumultuous history.

Man called the power God, Yahweh, Jehovah, Lord, Heavenly Father. . . .

From this great God power, immense love flowed to the human race, whom he had created in his own image. Over the centuries, God taught humankind about himself and his kingdom called heaven. Not only did he give man guidelines for living his life here on earth, but most importantly, God gave his plan for us to know him and have eternal life in his heavenly home.

It is within his plan that he asks us to live and die. Here we can find God's love. We can find his acceptance. We can find peace and joy and happiness.

We also will experience pain and sorrow, failure and discouragement. We live, after all, in a world that contains bad experiences and bad people. Good and bad things happen to all of us.

God's plan for us is found in God-breathed messages written by men over centuries of time. When combined together, we call them the Bible. It is one of two important ways God has chosen to reveal himself and his plan to humankind. In the Bible, God tells us how to live so we may honor and worship him. He tells us how we may have joy and peace and a life overflowing with his abundance. How we live is so important to God. It reflects our love for him and what he means to us as our God.

The answer to man's quest for eternal life is found in these Holy Scriptures. Within these God-inspired pages each of us can discover who we are and why we exist. Best of all, each of us can find how to have a relationship with the living God.

We know that vast numbers of people are religious or have a belief system that acknowledges some kind of god. Many people also view Christianity as a world-class religion. Yet, at the same time, they believe it is just one religion among many that can bring them to God or to whatever they may be seeking. They are certain that those who follow the procedures of other religions will be as heaven bound as a Christian. As a result, many choose to reject, in one form or another, the biblical way to know God.

There are numerous reasons offered by men and women today why some of the teachings of the Bible cannot be accepted. There is one reason, however, that we rarely discuss, hear about from the pulpit, or read in the literature. Whether this concern enters one's thinking process—consciously or subconsciously—it may be a major stumbling block to preventing many god believers from coming to a place in their lives where faith can take over and bring them into God's kingdom. This vital and very rational concern may produce enough doubt in a person's mind that it stops them from taking that final act of faith in completing their journey to God.

For the Christian believer, a lack of understanding of this fundamental concept of our faith may cause confusion in their belief system and in the quality of their faith. Failure to comprehend this vital doctrine of our Christian faith has the potential to create a vacuum, a blank space in an individual's capacity to believe the Christian gospel.

Think about it. Most people who live on Earth will not have access to God's word, the Bible. Nor will they hear its teaching in any meaningful way from anyone. How can they possibly know God's plan for life and death in their own lives?

What of the ancient cave dwellers, living millennia before the dawn of recorded history, or the Buddhist who worked on the Great Wall of China? Native Americans lived on the Great Plains of America long before the coming of the white man. Add to these the untold millions of people who have lived through the centuries never hearing the teachings in the Bible of God's redemptive gift of eternal life. Would God really reject all these people who have never heard of his plan to know him and live in his eternal home?

If the subject was discussed by a contemporary group of people selected at random, we might hear the following comments and questions. Perhaps you have thought or expressed such comments yourself.

"Is the way to heaven only found in the teachings of Christianity?"

"Is the religion of Jesus Christ the only religion that "works"?

"How can Christianity be for all the world's people when during the majority of human existence there was no Christianity?"

"Even from Christianity's beginnings there have been large people groups who have lived in the world and never heard of Jesus Christ."

"How can Christianity be the religion for everyone who has ever lived when most of them will never hear of God's plan?"

"Christianity is a rather localized religion for certain regions and people groups."

"How can God send people to hell who have never heard of Jesus?"

*Who Is Going to Heaven?* attempts to answer these questions and concerns. They are not answered by heavy theological arguments, but rather through the lives of mostly fictional men and women and the simple basic biblical truths taught in the Holy Scriptures.

It is important for us to always remember that the reality and teachings of God are never proved as in a court of law, but rather with many bits of evidence liberally mixed together with various amounts of our faith. God, through his Spirit, gives each of us who lived or ever will live enough faith to prove that he is real, to believe him, and to come into his Kingdom, if that is our desire.

Christianity is shown to be not just a religion existing during a portion of mankind's history in selected locations on earth. Rather, it is and has always been the encompassing structure by which God has chosen to bring all peoples from all strata of society and from all the ages of time into his kingdom. Its purpose is to proclaim that the power and intention of the Holy Spirit will assure that everyone who has ever lived or ever will live has the opportunity to come to an eternal relationship with God. This can be true even though the role of Jesus Christ in his salvation may be unknown or misunderstood.

It is the Christian, however, whom the Holy Spirit most desires to work through in bringing men and women into the kingdom of God. It is the evidence we share and the faith we demonstrate that enriches the work of the Holy Spirit in another person's life. It is the Christian's opportunity and life mission to demonstrate this evidence to an unbelieving world, and to express our faith that is so intangible, yet so real in our own lives.

We will also see how God is grieved when men and women strive and battle against one another. This is true whether the conflict is between Christians and unbelievers or among Christians themselves. Some of the stories examine the evil of the "man-against-man" syndrome prevailing in our human society and how it prevents the work of the Holy Spirit in the lives of both Christians and nonbelievers.

Human beings choose to response to God's leading in their lives intellectually and emotionally, and in varying amounts of each. Both are needed.

Evidence to lead the way.
Faith to complete the journey.
And the Holy Spirit blending the two together,
If we let him.

————•《O》•————

Part I, titled "Those Who Find Him," is a selection of short stories about the lives of people who never know of Jesus Christ or his part in God's plan, but who listen and respond to the leading of the Holy Spirit. They come from many differing circumstances and environments and from the whole spectrum of time in mankind's existence. They are the stories of God's gift of eternal life.

Part II, "The Shepherd Boy," is an ancient story about a little boy, who on a wonderful winter night many centuries ago, meets Jesus for the first time and finds his life changed forever. As his life intertwines with Christ and the Christian church, the boy grows to manhood and becomes a picture of the grace of God that exists for you and me.

Part III, "The Ways of God," shares God's loving plan for each of our lives. We can see that in life there are choices to be made about God and heaven, about life and death and eternity. God wants us to know his plan, because he desires each of us to live in his heaven forever.

So come now
And listen to their stories,
To their hopes and dreams.
Somewhere in time we can find ourselves.

# PART 1

## THOSE WHO FIND HIM

# ONE

## THE ARTIST

*By the later part of the twentieth century he had become a*
*World-renown artist*
*Featured in museums and art galleries all over the world.*
*His paintings had been published*
*In numerous upscale books and leading magazines.*

He grew up in southern France, and though he never traveled far from his place of birth, his ability to interpret his environment through painting had brought him great acclaim throughout the civilized world.

This creative, artistic man lived not in modern times, but many centuries before the dawn of recorded history. He was a cave dweller. For much of each year, he lived in one of the numerous caves from which his community hunted, fished, and harvested crops that grew wild in the forests and fields within a few miles of their homes.

When he had time, and even when he did not, he would paint beautiful stories on the walls of the caves.

In nearly every generation of human development, there appears on the scene unusual and gifted individuals who contribute greatly to the enrichment of their community, whether that community is local or worldwide. The Mozarts, Edisons, Platos, and Lincolns are scattered liberally throughout civilizations that have come and gone over the centuries of time.

And so, somewhere in time, and very long ago, on a beautiful summer morning, a baby boy was born.

Not unusual for this community. Many babies were born there. Many babies died there. The strongest and luckiest survived. This baby boy was strong and lucky. He had several things going for him. Within his world he had two healthy nurturing parents who showed him great love and attention, and four grandparents who were encouraging and always there for him. It was a nice combination not available to many children. Then again, many children do exceedingly well without such an ideal set of circumstances.

From somewhere in the past, a batch of genes was handed down to this baby, which brought him to a level of intellect considerably above his peers. As a young child, he was quick to pick up new ideas and learned rapidly the customs and skills needed to survive in a sometimes hostile environment. He related well with his peers, and very often helped them with the skills he had long since mastered. He excelled in the activities of young boys—running, wrestling, hunting small game, and tracking.

One cold winter day, when he was twelve years old, he did something that not only brought him to the attention of the clan leadership, but in a sense began to define the direction in which he was to live the rest his life.

For several weeks he had observed the headsman of his clan walking and performing his tasks with great difficulty and considerable pain. It was said he could not sleep at night and was always cold, no matter how many furs were piled on top of him. Many in the clan thought this might be the beginning of the end for their leader. He was forty-eight years old and had lived a rather long and good life. Perhaps it was his time.

For several days the boy thought about this dilemma that concerned his tribe. Then an idea came to him. On a day when the headsman was out hunting, he went to the area where his headsman slept and scraped out a hole about a foot deep, two feet wide, and five feet in length. It took him all morning for the floor of the cave was hard and filled with stones. When women of the clan questioned his activity, his smiling response that he was doing something for the headsman seemed to satisfy them.

After scraping out the hole, he built a framework of poles and vines so that a bedroll could be laid on top. He secured the framework on two short logs so that it rested about a foot above the hole. Then he built a tent like structure with poles and furs that completely surrounded the hole. It had a flap for a door and a hole at the top. Finally, he put the headsman's bedroll on top of the framework.

It was dusk when he finished and he knew the headsman and his hunting party would soon be returning. Right on time for supper they appeared. The bone, weary headsman did not see the structure before sitting down to eat his evening meal. As the headsman ate, the boy brought several containers of hot coals and dumped them into the hole. He closed the flap. Then he waited.

Approaching his bed area after his supper, the headsman stopped and stared at the structure in front of him for several moments. Carefully, he opened the flap and looked inside. Not lacking in wit, he asked if this had not been prepared for his cremation a little prematurely.

Then he asked who had built it. The little boy volunteered it was his doing and he explained what he hoped it would accomplish. The headsman stared at the boy and with a smile suggested he be the first to try it. Which the boy did, willingly, since he had already done so several times.

It was then the headsman's turn. Carefully climbing into his bedroll, he pulled the covers over himself and in a few minutes was asleep, snoring loudly to the relief of the boy and the others in the cave. Not until well after sunrise the next morning did he awaken, after his wife had inspected him numerous times throughout the night.

The softer bed and heat from the hot coals had kept the old headsman warm and comfortable. They did not cure his true ailments, but he thought they did, and the boy was suddenly a minor hero to the headsman and the entire clan. For the next few weeks there was much digging and building of similar contraptions by the people of the clan with advice from the little boy always readily available.

Over a period of time a strange phenomena occurred. Not only was the boy sought after for advice on the sleeping tent, but on other things as well. The people of the clan began to expect him to give advice and come up with solutions to some of the many problems the clan encountered. At the same time the boy began to view himself as one very capable of solving their problems, which he very often did, thanks to those special genes that had lifted him a notch or two above his clan in intelligence and common sense.

The boy found he liked to investigate his natural environment, from animals and plants to the movement of stars in the heavens. He also liked to solve mechanical problems. The women of the clan had to walk a steep path down to a fast-moving mountain stream to bring up water to the caves. After many days of thinking and planning, the boy rigged a pulley system of rope vines and buckets made of skins that would bring water from the mountain stream when cranked up from the top. He began raising and breeding rabbits and wild pigs in cages and pens, which helped stabilize the food supply during the lean times of the year.

And on and on it went, until by the time he was in his middle teens and nearly a man, he had become one of the most important leaders in the clan.

One day when he was in his eighteenth year, he came upon some women who were using various colored paints made from animal oils, various minerals, plants, and numerous other ingredients. They were decorating animal skins with designs familiar to the clan. For the first time in his life he became curious about the paints. And so during a period of several weeks, he became proficient in producing the various paint colors for himself. Exactly why he wanted to learn this skill he could not quite answer, even to himself.

He would remember the hunt the rest of his life, a hunt that had gone wrong, with a stampeding bison herd and the hunters caught in the open. He had thrown himself into a shallow ditch seconds before the frightened animals thundered over him.

He remembered the flair of their nostrils, their power-ful legs carrying those huge bodies galloping closer and closer to him. And before they jumped over his fragile place of safety, he saw the terror in their eyes. It was an experi-ence that would haunt him for months to come. Three of the clansmen had been killed and several hurt. It was the worse thing to happen to the clan in years.

Two nights later he had a dream, and in that dream he experienced the terror of the stampede all over again. He awoke during the middle of the night shaking and in a hot sweat. He laid there for a long time. Then rising from his bed, he lit a torch, gathered his paints, and went into the deepest part of the cave.

He found a smooth wall and then just stood and stared at it for a long while. Finally, he began to paint, awkwardly at first. But slowly and steadily forms of running animals began to appear, with all the physical and emotional en-ergy he remembered so vividly.

For many days he painted, stopping only to eat, rest, and mix his paints. It became his passion. Most other duties were left undone, much to the annoyance of his family and other members of the clan. Still, they let him paint, and in reality they were becoming more and more proud of the story his paintings were telling. They were beginning to like the idea of their past being told in such a vivid and permanent way.

And so he continued for years, this artist, this inventor, this Renaissance man of the Cro-Magnon era, enriching the lives of his clan and unknown to him, those who would live millennia later.

There was something else happening in his life, very subtly creeping into his mind and spirit. Doubts. Doubts of what he had been taught from the beginning of his youth. About the bear spirit for whom his clan was named. The gods of the harvest, the womb, the gods of fire, of the river. A multitude of gods for nearly every important item and occasion in their lives.

And yet when he looked at his world and the universe in space he saw order and logic in the movement of the stars and the sun and the moon. He saw purpose and reason in the changing seasons of the year, of planting, of growing, of harvesting. In living things, particularly, he saw the beauty and dynamics in each part of a human being or animal. And this is what he expressed so vividly in paintings on the walls of caves.

How did this all happen he would often wonder to himself? These living things, the heavens, the earth, and everything on the earth, operate with such precision and within such a complex system. He knew his world did not just fall into place. As an inventor, he knew that could not be. Some force was behind it all. This he knew for certain. But what kind of a force?

A living force? It had to be. Intelligence was needed to put all of this together! In other words, a god. "Oh no," he laughed, "not another god" But then the thought, what if there is really just one God?

And so, gradually, over time, the Holy Spirit taught the artist about God. Taught him because he was open to hearing the teaching of the Spirit. He heard the call of God faintly at first, but because there was no rebellion, his concept and idea of who God is became more and more accurate and real in his life.

Through the teaching of the Holy Spirit in his mind, heart, and soul, he began to think about sin and realize God's hatred of sin. He came to understand that he had sin in his life, and needed forgiveness for this sinful nature that was in him; that he needed to turn away from his sin and go the other way.

Gradually, he learned to pray, and when he became convinced that he needed forgiveness, he prayed and begged God to forgive him for being a man of sin and specifically for the sins of which he knew he was guilty.

As he prayed, he felt the weight and guilt of his sin leave his soul, and he knew he was free.

He often thought of his death. He prayed to God about death and what it meant. Was it all over then, when death came? No life beyond the grave? And again, the Holy Spirit taught him about heaven and his place in heaven as a child of God. He learned that God loved him with a love that was everlasting. And through this time of learning about God, he came to love him, and began to worship him as the Lord of his life.

He told the clan about his God. Although his people were not as fast to rid themselves of their various gods as they were to build themselves more comfortable bedsteads, over time a large portion of the clan became believers in the living God and worshiped him alone as their God.

For another two generations the artist led them in worship and taught them about the God of the universe. In later generations, over hundreds of years, the clan and other clans with whom they had shared the good news, worshiped the living God, and followed the leading of the Holy Spirit. Even though they could not identify him, they felt his power and presence in their lives. Their desire and willingness to follow the leading of God was, of course, not perfect nor total. But throughout these centuries God had the place of honor in their society. But their worship and dedication to the living God did not last forever.

Whenever parents or grandparents neglect to tell their children or grandchildren about God, and the principles under which they should live, there is great danger of succeeding generations failing to see the need of having a relationship with God and worshiping him. Sometimes, though, it is the children who rebel against the teaching of their parents, as well as against God, and then they fail to teach their children. In either situation the spiritual linkage of one generation to the next generation is then broken for that family, sometimes, forever.

When this occurs in enough families, the entire society breaks its link with spiritual concerns and with God. Sadly, over a few generations (🐾) this is what happened to the clans, who for a long time had worshiped God with such love and power. The light of God gradually dimmed and finally went out in their society.

In the Book of Exodus and the Book of Deuteronomy in the Old Testament of the Bible we find God, through his servant Moses, telling the Jewish people how to ensure that their children will hear the story of what God did for them and how he saved them. Here are some of his words of direction.

> When you are celebrating the Passover,
> And your children ask,
> "What does all this mean?

What is this ceremony all about?"
You will reply,
"It is the celebration of Jehovah's passing over us,
For he passed over the homes of the people of Israel,
Though he killed the Egyptians;
He passed over our houses and did not come in to destroy us."

and

O Israel, listen:
Jehovah is our God. Jehovah alone.
You must love him with all your heart, soul, and might.
You must think constantly about these commandments
I am giving you today.
You must teach them to your children
And talk about them when you are at home or out for
a walk;
At bedtime and the first thing in the morning.

Will we as parents and grandparents tell our children and grandchildren about God's love and his plan of salvation? Will our children listen and obey and come into God's family and pass the good news on to their children?

Will the linkage of generations, loving, worshiping, and serving God continue for your family? For my family? May it be so, for ever and ever.

How long ago this story could have taken place may be open to question, but certainly it was thousands of years ago, before any known organized religion was in existence in which the cave artist could have participated. And yet the Holy Spirit had the power and the desire even before the beginning of recorded history to reach down and call the artist and many in his community to God.

The men, women, and children who responded were cave dwellers, but cave dwellers called by God to everlasting life in heaven. Through the Holy Spirit's teaching and guidance they learned to love, worship, and obey God. They learned to seek his forgiveness. So when they died, their sins had been forgiven and they were welcomed into the kingdom of heaven.

Finally, when the old artist died on a beautiful summer morning, like one on which he was born, there was great personal sorrow by the clans people, but great rejoicing as well for the life of a man who loved and shared his God and was now in God's presence in heaven.

He had never known about Jesus,
But when he crossed over from his earthly life to his heavenly one,
He met him, as his Lord and savior for the first time.

# Two

## PEOPLE B.C.

For most cultures and societies, the time line of mankind's history is divided in two by its most important event, the coming of Jesus Christ in human form to Earth. The millennial year of 2000 A.D. is celebrated by nearly all the world's people, no matter what religion, if any, they may follow.

It is understandable, therefore, that historians would date the beginning of Christianity to the time Christ lived on earth, around two thousand years ago. On the basis of secular history, this is certainly correct. But viewed from true historical reality it is misleading.

For
In the beginning was Jesus Christ.
From the beginning of time
Christ was God,
Part of the trinity of God,
Father, Son, Holy Spirit.

Christianity existed from the beginning of time. It existed at creation as God created our world. There was Christianity when Adam and Eve committed the first sins of humankind. It was present when God sent the great flood to cleanse the world of its evil. When Noah and his family left the ark to repopulate the world, it was there. And when the time came for God to create his chosen people, the Jews, Christianity existed.

From Abraham, Isaac, and Jacob, the great patriarchs of the Jewish beginnings, to their migration from Egypt centuries later, with Moses and the great exodus into the Promised Land as the Israelites, there was Christianity. Always existing, always living, because Jesus Christ always lives.

Throughout Jewish history—the tabernacle and the ark of the covenant, the great temple built by Solomon, destroyed and rebuilt as the second temple, enlarged and made exceedingly beautiful by Herod, to the time of Christ's coming to earth as a Jew, and then on through the centuries, the Holocaust, and the reestablishment of the nation of Israel in 1948—the Jewish people existed and thrived under God's protection and love.

But always there was Christ, the Jew's Messiah, the savior of the world, not only to the Jews, but to all people.

But how could Jesus Christ, the savior of the world, be a savior before he died for our sins, before he came to earth as a man to die for our transgressions? How did men and women come to God before Christ came to die for them?

They came to God the same way people did after Christ's death: through faith, faith to believe God. Not just to believe in God, but to believe God.

When God told Abraham he would be the first of a new nation, a new people, his chosen people, Abraham had the faith to believe God. In Abraham God had found a person whose heart was his, one who recognized his sins and confessed them, and had the faith to believe that God would forgive him, that God was the true God of his universe and world, and he was to be Abraham's God.

And when Christ did die on the cross two thousand years later, he died for Abraham's sins, as well as the sins of all the men and women who had ever lived in the past from the time of Adam.

Cave dwellers in France
Nomads of the African desert
Sumerians
Egyptians
Moses
David and Solomon
Babylonians
Chinese farmers
Medes and Persians
Greeks
Socrates and Plato
Alexander the Great
Soldiers of his armies
Romans
Julius Caesar
Indian Buddhists
Builders of the Great Wall of China

All people before the time of Christ were visited by the Holy Spirit. All of them were able to see God through the wonderful creation he made of his world. They all had the opportunity and choice to know God to the extent the Holy Spirit had revealed God to them. All could acknowledge their sin and receive forgiveness from God's plan of redemption. Everyone had the opportunity to come into the kingdom of heaven when death took them from this earth.

Many made the right choice. But there were those who rejected God's calling, ignored the Holy Spirit's knocking, and entered an eternity without God.

# THREE

## THE WALL BUILDER

*As he trudged wearily up the steep incline*
*The thought came to the wall builder*
*That his existence was the least significant thing*
*Ever created on the face of the earth.*

Never was there a time when hopelessness was not his primary feeling. His life, all his life, had been manipulated or controlled by others. No self-direction had ever existed. He was as a puppet dangling down, waiting for the next movement from the hand above. But perhaps the cruelest part of his whole desperate life was his awareness of the depth of the tragedy and his inability to remove himself from its strangling grasp.

He carefully climbed the scaffold and placed the heavy stone where his mason could reach it, and began again the long hike to where he had come some twenty times

WHO IS GOING TO HEAVEN?

since daybreak. This he did day after day, and year after year, he and several thousand other builders in that small section of the

Wall,
The Great Wall,
The Great Wall of China.

It was now being reconstructed, made stronger, made invincible during the powerful but short-lived reign of the Sui Dynasty. Coming to power in 581 A.D., losing it thirty-seven years later in 617 A.D., this remarkable family brought together a disintegrated China and united it into a powerful nation. Part of the grand scheme of unification was a strong defense, which in turn placed the Great Wall as a vital component of that defense.

The beginnings of the Great Wall of China occurred in around 200 B.C., and during that century most of the wall had been built. There was reconstruction and enlargement of the wall between 386 A.D. and 534 A.D., during the Northern Wei dynasty. By the time the Sui Dynasty reconstruction had reached its peak, the wall had become a dazzling structure of both architectural dominance and a sometimes effective line of defense for the now unified China.

The wall stretched, weaving this way and then that way, up and then down and then up again, for more than three thousand miles from Shan Haikuan, on the Gulf of Peichili in eastern China, to Yumen of Kansu in far western China. Every two hundred yards there was a guard tower ready to send the signal of an attack to garrisons of soldiers strategically placed to quickly come and route an invader such as the likes of a Genghis Khan or other threatening armies.

He made many more trips that day. It was such back-breaking work. The stones were so heavy, and by dusk he could hardly lift one off the pile, which never seemed to shrink, no matter how many stones were removed. But he picked one up and carried the last one for the day up the steep path to the wall.

The climb up the scaffold was terrifying. Climbing down he fell the last five feet to the ground and lay stunned for several minutes until he finally stood up and trudged off toward his barracks and paltry evening meal. No one had tried to help him after his fall. He knew no one would. No one ever did.

He was not a slave exactly. He was a volunteer. Not really a volunteer, actually, since it was the head of his village who had volunteered him five years ago when he was sixteen years old, when army units had come to the village seeking "volunteers." So he thought of himself as a volunteer, even though he knew he was not.

He dreamed of leaving the wall when it was finished and getting on with his life somewhere. They had promised him this, someday.

He lay on his bedroll that night, so tired and tense that he could not fall asleep in a few seconds like he usually did. He thought of his life. His parents dead of a fever when he was four years old. Relatives, and not nice ones, took him in, and worked him immediately in the fields until he was twelve. Little to eat or wear, and hardly any free time for himself. Slave work it really was. And he hated them.

Hated them with a fury. When he would lash out they would beat him. Beat him until he was as a whimpering dog.

When they rented him out to a well-to-do farmer down the road he felt his first happy moment in memory. That was a mistake. He knew it five minutes after he arrived. For four years he endured not only harder work and longer hours, but also humiliation in front of those with whom he worked, through beatings and scornful mocking. He was a small boy and easy to pick on.

So when the army came and took him away, marching, he had a sense of great excitement. Perhaps his new life would be better than his past sixteen years. For a while it was. He did meet people with whom he could talk and have a relationship. Slowly but surely, however, the intensity and the amount of work expected of the labor force wore them down until they were like hungry and desperate animals, concerned only with survival, making it one day to the next.

The wall builder was a Buddhist. He could tell anyone who asked which religion he belonged to: He was a Buddhist. No one had ever asked, but that would be his answer if they did. He had never been taught about Buddhism. And what he did know about it had been picked up randomly from conversations overheard at different times and scattered throughout his young life. But with all the bits and pieces he knew about his religion, he would be hard pressed to explain to anyone, even in the simplest way, the religion of Buddhism. If anybody had asked.

Accidents were always happening at the wall. It was a very dangerous place. Men falling. Stones falling. Hurting, dying. It was a very tricky place to stay alive and well. And no one cared whether you lived or died, were maimed or remained whole. There were always more to replace you. The wall was the only thing that mattered. Life was on the cheap at the wall. Badly hurt? You're on your own. You volunteered, remember? Better off if you just die and not bother with all the suffering and dying.

It was dusk. Nearly time to end another day's work, eat some slop, say a few complaining words to a barracks mate, then to bed, again exhausted and feeling like death was close and maybe welcome. The wall builder heard a scream, saw a body falling from the wall and land in a pile of dirt a few feet away. The man lay motionless. Then in a few moments the body moved slightly. The wall builder started over to him.

A foreman yelled at him to get back to work. So down the trail he went to pick up his last stone for the day.

When he returned the man still lay on the mound of dirt, with moaning sounds and twitching and frightened eyes. The wall builder came over to the suffering body and asked, "If I help you, can you get up?" The hurting man nodded in desperation. The man knew that this offer of help was his last chance. He would die for sure in the cold night fast approaching. The wall builder bent down and pulled the groaning, shaking man to his feet. Together they stumbled down the hill to the barracks of the wall builder.

The wall builder knew very little about sickness and injury and death, but he could see death on his bed pad and fast approaching, too. Walk away and let him die, he thought. But something deep within him rebelled and he said, "No, I'll stay. He needs someone to die with. He needs some comfort. I can give him that."

And so he brought water to the dying man, whose lips were dry and thirsty. When he had given him all he needed to drink, he saw tears in the man's eyes and heard a "thank you" from the man's lips. The wall builder nodded and turned away.

When it was time for the evening ration, he left the dying man and went to get his slim amount of food. Instead of sitting on the ground and grumbling with his fellow workers, he brought the food back to his bed pad and shared it with the injured man. The injured man was grateful but could eat very little, and that amount made him sick so he could eat no more.

As the wall builder ate the remains of the meal, he began to shiver for the cold wind was whipping through the poorly constructed barracks. It was then he noticed for the first time the injured man was not wearing his coat and he too was shivering, even more than himself. When asked where it was, the man told him the foreman had taken it as he lay helpless on the pile of dirt. The foreman had laughed and told him that he would not need it where he was going.

Great sorrow overcame the wall builder. He thought to himself, "Why are humans like that? Is there no good in us at all?"

Then he took off his own coat, his only coat, and wrapped it around the dying man and the shivering began to lessen. He saw a smile and a soft "thank you" reached his hearing and his heart. As the night moved through its dark, long hours, the wall builder became very cold and suffered terribly, waking, dozing, always cold, horribly cold.

The last hours before dawn and rising time he slept fitfully. As he awoke, he heard the man cough and choke. Then he felt the touch of the man's hand on his, and heard him say very faintly, "Thank you my good and faithful friend." Then his eyes closed and he was dead.

At that very same moment, but thousands of miles away at a monastery in a mountainous region, in what is now northern Italy, a monk sat hunched over his writing desk, copying a portion of the Holy Scriptures from the Gospel according to the Apostle Matthew. In this sobering prophecy he was writing the words of Jesus.

But when I, the Messiah, shall come in my glory,
And all the angels with me,
Then I shall sit upon my throne of glory.
And all nations shall be gathered before me.
And I will separate the people as a shepherd separates
the sheep from the goats,
And place the sheep at my right hand, and the goats at
my left.
Then I, the King, shall say to those at my right,
"Come, blessed of my Father, into the Kingdom prepared
for you
From the founding of the world.
For I was hungry and you fed me;
I was thirsty and you gave me water;
I was a stranger and you invited me into your homes;
Naked and you clothed me;
Sick and in prison, and you visited me.'
Then these righteous ones will reply,
"Sir, when did we ever see you hungry and feed you?
Or thirsty and give you anything to drink?
Or a stranger, and help you?
Or naked, and clothe you?

When did we ever see you sick and in prison, and visit
you?'
And I, the King, will tell them,
"When you did it to these my brothers you were doing
it to me!'
Then I will turn to the ones on my left and say,
"Away with you, you cursed ones,
Into the eternal fire prepared for the devil and his de-
mons. . . .'
"When you refused to help the least of these my broth-
ers,
You were refusing to help me,'
And they shall go away into eternal punishment;
But the righteous into everlasting life.

The wall builder stared in sorrow and shock at the dark
form of the dead man. But his next thought was what he
should do with the body that was lying there among the
soon-to-be-awakened men. They would not think kindly
that a dead man was sleeping in their barracks! In a moment or two he had made his decision.

Finding a shovel, he went to a secluded place near a
completed section of the wall and dug a shallow grave.
Hurrying back to the barracks, he lifted the body in his
arms and carried it back to the grave where, with as much
dignity as possible, he placed it in the hole he had dug.
Then he filled in the grave and placed rocks on top. Missing his morning rations, he hurried to his job site where
his foreman soundly beat him for being late.

Even so, throughout the whole day of terrible exhaus-
tive work, he felt a strange emotion he had never experienced before. It was one of knowing he had done the right

thing by helping someone in need. Even more, he had attached himself to someone in an emotional and meaningful way. This he had never done before in his entire life. He knew that and what he felt was very good.

That evening he went into a nearby woods and hacked off a tree branch. From it he cut off two straight pieces about three inches in diameter. He then tied them together near the middle so they were perpendicular to each other. Carrying the two connected wood pieces to the grave he dug a small hole and placed the longest wood piece upright in the hole. He packed in the soil around it.

Why he had done this he was not quite sure. Somehow he just felt it was the right thing to do, a sign of respect, a remembrance of a life, a marking of a scared spot. Maybe something even more, but he did not really know what it was.

But as he left the grave and returned to his barracks, he felt good about himself, better than he could ever remember. Before he slept he thought about his life. Was this all there was to be of it, what he had experienced the last twenty-one years? Until today he had experienced hardly anything in his life that was good and meaningful. Why had this man come into his life for those few hours? Why did he feel so good about what he did for him?

Then he thought about his own death. It would come someday. Would there be life beyond the hole in the ground? Is there a place one goes to, his soul goes to? He wondered about a supreme God. What did his future hold? He wished he knew. He almost whispered to God, if there was one, concerning what was ahead of him in life and death. He did not quite do it, but he did think it. Then he slept.

That night he dreamed. He dreamed he was in a city, a holy city. He saw it was the home of the living and only true God. It seemed filled with the glory of God and it glowed like a precious gem. He saw that its walls were very broad and high, with twelve gates guarded by twelve angels. The city was shaped like a giant cube. Its height, width, and length were fifteen hundred miles each way. The city itself was made of pure, transparent goldlike glass. The walls were made of jasper and the twelve gates made of pearls.

The wall builder saw no temple in the city, for he learned in his dream that the holy and living God and the Lamb of God were worshiped everywhere. He found the city had no need of the sun or moon for light, for the glory of God and his son illuminated it.

He thought it was such a wonderful place, for he saw not only its beauty and its richness, but discovered there would be no more death, nor sorrow, nor crying, nor pain. All of that would be gone forever. God would wipe all the tears from his eyes.

Then in the distance he saw a bright light, brighter than the sun itself. As he moved closer and closer to the light, it seemed to fade and pull away from him. He wondered why this was happening, since he very much wanted to be near this light.

Then in his dream he discovered that in the Holy City, the dwelling place of the living God,

Nothing evil will be permitted in it, . . .
But only those whose names are written in the
Lamb's Book of Life.

And when he heard this his dream shattered, and he awoke shaking and with great sobbing tremors. As he lay awake in the dark hours of the morning, the dream, instead of fading as dreams usually do, became more real and vivid in his mind. His one consuming desire, as he lay there in the darkness, was that he would live forever in that wonderful place he had just visited.

But he had learned no evil would be permitted there, and he knew there was evil in himself. He hated. He hated nearly everyone he ever knew. He could recognize this as evil after being in the Holy City, even if it were only a dream. He was a bitter, angry person. And that, too, he could now recognize as evil. He then remembered how very selfish he really was, always trying to maneuver more than his share of the food rationed out each day. He would steal when he thought he would not get caught.

In his value system, which, until now, was nearly nonexistent, he recognized all these things were evil and would keep him out of this wonderful and holy place. And so, as he does with all whose hearts are open to him, the Holy Spirit continued with great love and power to guide the wall builder. Into his mind, heart, and soul came the desire to talk to this God who ruled this city in which he wished to live forever. And so he did.

There in the darkness he began talking to the living God. Haltingly at first, but then with desperate pleadings, that his evil would be forgotten and he would be allowed to live forever in that beautiful place he had visited in his dream. For a long while he pleaded with God, talking about the evil things in his life, talking about the evil he knew was in him, asking that the sin in his life be taken out and not held against him.

Finally, he said to God, "Whatever this Lamb's Book of Life is, I want my name written in it." And when he prayed that prayer he had peace he had never felt before. He knew he would be safe when he died. He would be part of that beautiful city, the Holy City of the living God and the Lamb of God.

If anyone that wonderful day had asked the wall builder if he were a Buddhist, he would have said that he was, for being a Buddhist, or a Hindu, or a Baptist, or a Lutheran, or a Roman Catholic, or any other religion, can often be part of one's cultural heritage, and not truly be part of one's faith or belief system, if one exists at all. He might have added with great excitement, that he had talked with the living God, and he was going to live in his Holy City when he died! But no one asked him.

There are many reasons why people die when they are young. God is responsible for some of them. And for some of the reasons he is not the cause at all. He may hate the death more than anyone.

It is difficult to know why the wall builder died on that wonderful day when his sins had been forgotten, the day he knew he would live forever with his God. Perhaps he was careless and slipped, or accidentally jostled. A part of the scaffold might have worn out and broke. Or God may have decided he had suffered enough in his earthly life, or may have seen horrific times ahead for him. It may have been the coming together of God's great love for the wall builder and the wall builder's great desire to be in God's presence and in the Holy City.

It was late afternoon when he fell, just after bringing up another heavy stone. He turned and stepped back onto the scaffold and he fell, fell from the top of the Great Wall of China, banging down through the scaffolding, breaking arms, legs, and neck, and dead before hitting the rocky ground below.

"Get that body out of here!" the foreman yelled, pointing to two of his workers. "Take him down about fifty yards to that hole in the wall and toss him in before they seal it up. Hurry now!"

So the two men dragged the bleeding and broken body to the hole under repair and threw the wall builder into it. Then without looking at his body for even a moment, turned and walked back to their work. Within the hour the grave of the wall builder had been sealed.

To the world he was gone, forgotten, a speck of nothing. Perhaps to the world his existence really was the least significant thing ever created on the face of the earth. In a few months his body would decay, eventually turn to dust and return to the earth.

But halfway down the scaffolding the greatest of all the miracles of God occurred. For when physical death came, the wall builder's eternal life that had begun that very day continued forever in the Holy City of God.

And in the very moment he died, he saw in the distance a light brighter than the brightest of suns. As he walked toward its magnificent brilliance, the light did not fade or pull away as it did in the dream, but moved toward him until it surrounded his entire being.

Then he saw Jesus, the Lamb of God, for the first time. And though he had never heard of the name "Jesus" in his earthly life, when he met him face to face in the Holy City, he knew that he was his savior and his Lord.

Falling on his knees he bowed in worship. Jesus put his hand on the wall builder's head and spoke to him.

"I was thirsty and you gave me water to drink.
I was hungry and you fed me.
I was cold and you gave me your coat.
You did all these things for me.
Now welcome home,
My deeply loved and worthy friend,
You will rule with me in my Kingdom,
Forever and ever."

# FOUR

## THE MOSLEM WOMAN

*In the year 1099 A.D. in the city of Jerusalem,*
*A man lay near death in his own house,*
*While his wife in desperation cared for his wounds.*
*He had been brought there that evening by friends*
*Who with him had fought a great battle*
*With the Christian crusaders from western Europe.*

As she cared for him, great anger flooded her mind and heart. Anger toward her own religion, Islam, but much more anger and hatred toward the bloody religion of Christianity, under whose name the European barbarians had attacked her city and may have mortally wounded her husband and her way of life.

It was not that she failed to believe in a god. She did. But that evening she decided in her bitterness that the god in which she believed was not her old Islamic god who had been so harsh, violent, and unforgiving all her life. And it certainly could never be a bloody and cruel god like the Christian's god who seemingly was about to take her husband from her.

During the many days and nights that followed, her prayers were simple and unyielding. As she cared for her husband through her weariness and exhaustion, she prayed. She prayed that the true God of her earth and heaven, whoever he was, would save her husband and show himself to her so that she could believe in the right God. She prayed this over and over, day after day, night after night.

The Bible is very clear on this. When one calls on God to reveal himself, and that prayer is honest and without wrong agendas, God has promised he will respond. He will begin to enter the life of that person. In the Old Testament, King David told his son Solomon,

> The Lord sees every heart and understands and knows every thought.
> If you seek him you will find him,
> But if you forsake him, he will permanently throw you aside.

And so the Holy Spirit began to show her the true God of her life and she began to experience his great love and comfort. Over time he revealed to her much of the character of her new, great God.

But there was something very wrong. She knew sin still existed in her life. No matter how hard she tried to fight against it, the sin would not leave. No matter how good a person she tried to be, it still remained. She also believed that a holy and good God would not want that sin in his paradise. She sensed that very clearly. But yet she desperately wanted to be in his presence, now and when she died.

As the days passed, two momentous things happened in her life. First her husband, who had progressively worsened since returning home, began to recover, and though still very ill, appeared to be out of danger of death. For that she profusely thanked her new and now much-appreciated God over and over again.

But there was still a mighty danger not far from her door. The fighting was getting closer and reports indicated her people were losing the battle and the city to the crusaders. Perhaps it was her fear of imminent death that motivated her decision. But in addition to this great fear of death, the leading of the Holy Spirit also had brought direction and hope to her mind, heart, and soul.

So as she heard the noise of battle grow closer, she lay prone on the floor of her home and begged her new God to forgive the sins she had tried so hard to rid of herself. She pleaded with him to take her into his paradise when she died. As she prayed, a peace she had never experienced before came into her life and she knew her God had forgiven her and would take her into his heavenly home when she died, whether it was that day or in the years to come.

She survived the war and her husband did recover. Over the years she grew closer to her God as she listened to the Holy Spirit teach and guide her.

Many years after she had truly come to belong to God, and even though greatly isolated from Christianity, she did come to the knowledge that Jesus Christ was the Christians' savior from sin. Over time the Holy Spirit gently led her to think that perhaps Jesus was her savior, too.

And so one day, later in life, and perhaps a little grudgingly, she obeyed the Holy Spirit's leading and prayed these words: "Merciful God, if Jesus is the savior of the world, let him be my savior, too." With that prayer came peace, and she was satisfied that she had done the right thing.

Soon after the battle she told her husband and children about her God and new faith, but they rebuked her strongly and she was very saddened by this. But over the years she made her home a place she knew would please her God, and a place of security and happiness for her family.

In the forty-one years she lived from the time she found the right God, she carefully shared her faith with numerous women she knew, and two came to know her God as she had.

She knew Jesus very faintly as her savior, but he was still her savior. He died for her sins, and without his sacrifice on the cross her sins could not have been forgiven by God.

So her earthly journey ended in heaven, where she too met Jesus and knew she had made the right choice. God had found a person whose heart was open and he led her to paradise.

# FIVE

## THE APACHE WARRIOR

*Far in the distant past on the Great Plains of southwest*
*North America,*
*There lived nomadic tribes of warriors,*
*Who in the centuries to follow would be called Apaches.*
*It was a time before the Europeans had come to their lands,*
*Before the age of Columbus and explorers like Coronado,*
*And then all the rest who were to follow,*
*Coming to change the lives of Native Americans forever.*

But on a warm May evening, and a very long time ago
in the year 1443 A.D., one of these Apache warriors trudged
wearily to a clump of trees where he hoped to spend the
night in quiet rest. It had been a long, hot day's walk, and
his exhaustion was severely testing his body and spirit. He
had been away from his tribe and family for many days and
was anxious to sit by his familiar campfire with family

around him. Besides that, he was traveling alone. Not only was this dangerous but also lonely, and he was one who enjoyed being with his people.

As he built a small fire to cook his meager meal—a small rabbit he had killed a few hours before—he began to hum a simple tune. He had sung it many times since he first heard his mother sing it as she held him in her arms many years ago. It spoke of their gods and how their relationship with these gods depended on sacrifices made, or acts of homage, or pain suffered, or performing special feats of bravery. He hummed it without thinking of the words that belonged to the tune. But it brought to him warm thoughts of home and that was what he needed right then, as night shadows began to fall on the great desolate plains so huge that one felt swallowed up in the immensity of their vastness.

After the rabbit was devoured, along with some wild berries he had picked on his long day's march, he kicked out the small cooking fire, wrapped himself in a thin bedroll and within a few moments fell into a deep sleep. For several hours he slept. Whether it was a coyote's howl or the scream of a hyena in the distance, something awakened him, and rather abruptly, too. In an instant he grabbed his war hatchet and spun around in all directions, swinging his deadly club savagely in the air, while at the same time tripping clumsily over his bedroll. Seeing he was not under attack, he gradually relaxed. A slight smile came to his lips as he thought how fortunate he was that no one in his tribe had observed his frantic awakening. He stood very still while his breathing quieted. It was during these moments that he realized how completely the stillness of the dark night had overtaken him with loneliness and the urgency to know the purpose of his existence and where it would end.

The warrior believed in the things of the spirit. He and his tribe had many gods, a god for most of the meaningful things in their lives and society. But on this very night, as stars shone down on his earth, he began to wonder and ponder once again about the reality of his god system. On what was it really based? Oh, he knew the stories and legends that had passed through the generations. But was it real? He had done much pondering over the past weeks and months about his gods. They seemed to be so loosely connected. Rather petty, and not what he had begun to perceive would be the characteristics of a real god.

Those thousands of stars. Where did they really come from? His earth, the animals, his people, and himself? When and how did they first begin? It was at that moment, as he looked into the sparkling heavens, this Indian warrior saw for the first time the need to believe only one great and powerful God could be the maker of all this world in which he existed.

And so before the dawn brightened the eastern sky, the young Apache became a one-God believer, intellectually rejecting the tribal concept of multiple gods.

Would this astonishing conclusion have brought him into a true relationship with the living God of his universe? The answer has to be no, but it was a beginning. God's great creative and complex world had led him to believe that there was but one God. His concept and ideas of God and who he really is may have been very inaccurate. But his acceptance of one God as his creator was central in beginning a process that would finally bring him to God and into God's family.

As the Apache observed God's creation, why did he come to believe that there was a single, powerful God who had created his universe and his own life? Deep inside his being he heard  the Holy Spirit gently calling to his mind, heart and soul, revealing to him truth, giving him direction, and guiding his life.

His response was to accept the truth revealed to him. He had begun moving in the right direction and making right choices. And by accepting the Holy Spirit's call, the warrior prevented a layer of hardness from covering his soul and prepared himself for the continued gentle leading of the Holy Spirit.

Perhaps it can be believed that, if this Apache warrior had died before the morning sun had reached the horizon after that lonely night, God would have received him into his kingdom. For the warrior had not rejected the call of the Holy Spirit in his life that night, but rather followed his leading. Or it may be that God would never allow one of his children to enter a heavenless eternity, if they were obeying the Spirit's call to the extent they were capable of obeying.

But the warrior did reach his home fires before the next sundown. In the weeks that followed he thought much about this great God who created and influenced his world. As he did, the Holy Spirit guided his thinking and these new concepts, and his understanding of God became clearer and more realistic and valid. Gradually, the God he believed in became very real in his life. He was making the right choices as he obeyed the call of the Holy Spirit in his life.

One cold, sunlit morning in early winter, the warrior was hunting alone a few miles from his village. From a deep ravine a party of warriors from an unfriendly tribe suddenly came around a large outcropping of rock. Great fear came over him. Death seemed to be certain, for there would be no mercy from this tribe. This he knew. Suddenly, into his mind came a desire to do something he had never done before. He prayed to the living God. Actually, he screamed out silently, "Help me, great God! Help me!" At that moment a miracle seemingly occurred, for the enemy warriors, as if they were blinded, passed him by. Overwhelmed by his good fortune the warrior whispered, "Thank you, mighty God, thank you." Again he had made a right choice.

In the days that followed, the warrior began having troubling thoughts about many of the things he was doing in his daily life. Whenever he worshipped the great lion spirit, the strangest feeling of sadness came over him and bothered him greatly. As he thought about this feeling he had never experienced before, there came to his understanding the obvious reason he felt this way. Why should he be worshiping a god that really did not exist when there was but one God?

Cruel treatment of captive slaves was long an excepted practice within his tribal society. His participation of the tormenting process began to greatly bother him, even though it was expected by those in his tribe and even among the slaves themselves.

His bad temper was earning him a reputation among tribal members, but even so, within the mores of his society, was not considered to be so bad a quality for a warrior to possess. Gradually, however, he began to realize deep within his mind and soul that these lifestyle characteristics were wrong and would not please his new and singular God.

Feelings of guilt began to assault him day after day. Finally, in desperation he cried out to God to help him again.

He prayed to God to take these wrong things out of his life. Slowly things did change. He no longer worshiped the lion god, though admittedly, he still went through the act of doing so for a good while longer. He completely stopped his cruel treatment of captive slaves. In fact cruelty was replaced by kindness. But what surprised the young warrior the most was that the control of his temper was gradually improving.

So once again the Apache warrior had responded to the Holy Spirit's leading and felt guilt in his soul for these sins, and then made the right choice when he asked God to take them out of his life.

Then into his mind came the thought of his death. What would his new and great God do with his soul when he died? He began to realize there were still wrong things occurring in his life, and this God he was beginning to know was a holy and righteous God. How could he enter into his presence when he died with all these wrong things that were such a part of his life.

For many days he struggled with this frightening thought. Finally, he knew he would have to go to his God and beg forgiveness for the wrong things that made up his life. He knew he would never be able to take them away himself. And so, before he slept that night, he cried out to God, admitting his sins, begging his forgiveness, and asking the Lord of his world to take him into his presence when he died. At that moment a miracle occurred. The Apache warrior became a child of God. He received eternal life, to be welcomed into heaven when he died by a loving Lord.

Did this warrior think up these concepts of sin, death, the hereafter, and God as a holy God? No, the Holy Spirit's urging and teaching produced them in his mind, heart, and soul. The warrior did not turn back the Holy Spirit's call. He had made the right choice.

And obviously, throughout this entire process of coming to God, including the final act of calling to God for mercy for his sins and his acceptance into God's presence when he died, the warrior could never have heard of Jesus Christ, God's son, and his sacrifice on the cross for his sins. Yet it was still Christ's sacrifice that made possible his salvation. Christ's death on the cross still paid for his sins for which he had asked to be forgiven. Without Christ's sacrifice he could not have come to God in any way. Christ was the answer to his life and his salvation. He just did not know anything about it.

As time passed the Apache warrior often told his friends about this one God he prayed to and trusted. Many listened because they respected him as a member of their tribe. But most rejected this strange idea of one true and merciful God. Even so, numerous members of his tribe over the years did come to know the warrior's God and had much the same peace in their lives.

Even though most of the tribe continued as before in worship of many gods, the influence of those who had accepted the warrior's God changed the tribe. Many of its decisions now centered on concepts of behavior that made the tribe a better place for all to live. There seemed to be more peace and tolerance and kindness in the community.

The warrior did not live a perfect life, of course. He still sinned and he knew he did. But when sin came into his life, he was able to pray for forgiveness from his God.

The years passed and the Apache warrior's faith and love for his great God continued to grow. Long past the time death came to most, the old warrior became ill and gathered his family around him for the last time. He told them once again how he had come to know the great God of the universe, now his personal God whom he would soon see.

Early the next morning as the sun begin to rise in the eastern sky, the ancient warrior died and entered his heavenly home. It was there he met Jesus for the first time and he knew why he was home.

# SIX

## THE JEWISH SCHOLAR

*He had been in combat for five horrible days*
*And it had been very bloody and dirty and hard.*
*The killings were brutal and devastating to*
*Everything he valued*
*And felt sacred about life.*
*Yet he had killed close up and personally.*
*He saw the faces that died.*
*He was nineteen.*
*So young to kill.*
*Too young to die.*

They entered the old city through the Dung Gate, he and his infantry company. Advancing from building to building, darting from one place of cover to another, they received sporadic small arms fire from the Jordanian troops who had controlled the city and were now desperately attempting to defend it.

Suddenly the young soldier realized he was alone. He had been in front of his company's advance and somehow had taken a wrong turn in the confused maze of narrow and dark streets that intermingled with each other as they wove through the ancient city. He now became even more frightened but still forced himself to move on, slowly and carefully, from one building to another, seeking as much cover as possible from the death that would surely come if exposed to an enemy rifleman. Finally, he came to a corner of an ancient building. Peering around it he saw the most astounding sight he had ever encountered.

His father had told him about it as a young child. His life had centered around its meaning as he grew up. Two hundred feet away he saw a portion of the wall, the original wall that had encompassed the ancient temple of Jewish worship, and was destroyed by the Romans nineteen hundred years before.

The Western Wall of the Temple Mount
The Jewish Wailing Wall
At
Jerusalem, Israel

Alone and oblivious to the danger of enemy fire, the soldier slowly walked toward the wall in stunned amazement, through rubble and debris accumulated over years of Jordanian occupation. As he came closer he was overwhelmed by the sacredness of the place. The hope of religious Jews the world over was to worship there once again. This he knew, and it astounded him to think he was there completely alone. As he walked closer and closer it seemed he was approaching God instead of a wall.

He slung his rifle and touched the wall with both hands, leaned against it and tried to pray to God, but no words would come. Only tears of joy flooding his face and his soul.

Peace did come to Israel for a few years in June of 1967. The holy city came under complete Jewish control for the first time in more than twenty-one hundred years. The soldier went home and became part civilian, part soldier. He would fight again. He entered the Hebrew University of Jerusalem and studied history and philosophy. He also began immersing his mind with his Jewish history and religion. He studied the Torah. He married and had a son whom they named David.

He was a religious Jew, rather orthodox in his beliefs, although if he tried to pin himself down, and he did so on many occasions, it seemed difficult for him to develop a cohesive set of beliefs that fit together and satisfied both his mind and his soul. He did believe there was a God, one more God than many of his friends believed in.

The reality of sin was something else in which he believed very strongly. He knew it existed in the world, with all its evil and war and cruelty. It certainly had existed in Germany and Eastern Europe during World War II.

In the Camps
In the Camps
In the Camps

Because of the terrible sin in those places of evil he had almost not existed. But where does sin really exist? He had thought a great deal about this for many months.

Are sin and evil just floating around out there in the world, on his old battlefields, over Germany, at his grandparent's Auschwitz, in Cairo, and other enemy ports of call?

Where is sin's home? Where does it live? Slowly the answer entered his thinking that sin exists only in the minds and hearts and souls of individual people. There is no other place for sin to live.

At the same time he was looking inward at his own life. He knew he had sinned many times. In fact he could make quite a list, he thought with a smile. But with that smile and past remembrances came thoughts of how serious sin was to his God of the Old Testament, and how displeased God was when his chosen people, the Jews, sinned so many centuries ago.

Could God be any less concerned about sin today? He knew the answer and it made him wonder about his own sins and what God thought of them and even more unsettling what God would do about them. As he pondered these concerns, the scholar found himself discovering new thoughts about his holy God as the Holy Spirit gently gave them to him. He was determined not to be against this new way of thinking about God and himself. Perhaps without realizing it, he was considering the Spirit's truths through very carefully. He was making right choices. God had found an open heart.

Before the Romans destroyed the temple and the Jews scattered from Jerusalem in 70 A.D., there were daily animal sacrifices at the temple. Centuries before God had commanded Abraham and the Jews to shed the blood of animals for the atonement of their sins. The animals were sacrificed on the temple altar so God could forgive the sins of the people. God's forgiveness always requires the shedding of blood.

But for more than nineteen hundred years there had been no means for the Jews to offer sacrifices for their sins, because this can only be done in the holy temple and it had been destroyed. This is why religious Jews pray at the Wailing Wall, the western wall of the Temple Mount. They pray for their Messiah to come and restore his temple once again, so their sins can be forgiven by the shedding of blood.

So the young Jewish scholar came more and more frequently to the sacred wall. His great desire was to pray for the Messiah to come and rebuild the Jewish temple so sacrifices for sins could be made for himself and his people. Deep in his heart and soul he had a great need to be forgiven for his sins, and he expressed this to God as he prayed day after day. As he did, the Holy Spirit worked in his life, and even though he thought his Messiah had not yet come, he had forgiveness from God. And slowly he began to feel the weight of his sin leave his soul and he knew he was free and belonged to his heavenly Father.

Why was God able to forgive his sin? Because his Messiah had come to earth in the man Jesus. Jesus Christ had died on the cross and shed his blood as an offering to God for the sins of the world and the sins of this Jewish man.

The young scholar knew he was a sinner and needed his sins to be forgiven. He had told God this many times. And he believed the Messiah was the one who would make this possible. He did not believe his Messiah would die for his sins, but when he returned he would provide the way for them to be forgiven through the blood sacrifice of animals at the altar of the restored temple. Although he believed that his Messiah had not yet come, he still believed in Messiah and that is where he placed his faith.

In his mind and heart he believed some things that were wrong and inaccurate. But because of his most vital beliefs—that of recognizing his sin, confessing them to God, and believing the Messiah to be the one who would provide the way of sacrifice for his sin—God was able to reach into his soul and remove his sin and bring him into his kingdom for ever and ever.

Culturally he was unable to recognize Jesus Christ as his Messiah. Perhaps in time the Holy Spirit would have shown him the truth. However, the scholar had opened his heart to his Lord God to the extent he was capable. He had made the right choice. God had found a man that was his.

Except for the assurance we can all have of our own relationship with God, we really do not know for certain, as we live our lives here on this earth, who will accept Christ's gift of eternal life. God's grace is capable of being received by some who we may feel do not have it "right" with God. Perhaps their outward appearance or beliefs, not quite like our own, may have convinced us they could not be God's children. But those who come to God with an open and contrite heart, desiring God's mercy and his life eternal will be led by the powerful Spirit of God to that eternal life.

Years passed and there was war again in Israel. On Yom Kippur, the holiest of Jewish days, October 6, 1973, Israel was attacked by Egypt and Syria.

The holy day of Yom Kippur is the Day of Atonement for the Jewish people. On that day they confess to God their sins they committed during the past year and offer prayers of forgiveness for these sins. When the holy temple existed, the high priest would enter the Holy of Holies in the temple to offer a blood sacrifice for the sins of the people. Then a goat called the scapegoat would be driven into the desert, symbolizing the carrying away of the sins of the Jewish people.

It was on this day that the Israelis went to fight and die. The scholar, now twenty-three years old and a company commander, led his men in defense of the Golan Heights against Syrian attacks. The attack had come without warning and he and his company were rushed in to head off the onslaught.

For several hours on that holy day they fought in bloody combat. Then, in a short firefight in the late afternoon, the young Jewish scholar was killed. As he lay dying, his last thought on earth was a prayer to God that his Messiah would soon come.

And as his earthly life flowed from him, he saw a great light and heard the singing of angels as he was ushered into his heavenly home. Coming toward him was Jesus, whom he could now recognize as the one who had saved him and paid the blood offering for his sins.

He was home and he had met his Messiah.

# SEVEN

## THE GANG BANGER

*In the darkness of the early morning hours*
*He was finding sleep close to impossible.*
*Yet he knew he needed sleep if he were to*
*Function well the following day,*
*One of the most important days in his life.*

No position in which he maneuvered his body did he feel the comfort that would finally cause his mind to doze off into any level of sleep. So he stayed awake, helpless in his dilemma. In reality it was not a total dilemma, for he often enjoyed laying awake at night, thinking about people and events and conflicts that went on in his daily, turbulent life.

But this night was to be different, for he found his mind being bombarded by thoughts of the past, the distant past, when he was a little boy.

He could not actually remember when he was two years old, but he did remember the stories he was told, very often as a matter of fact, by his mother and grandmother. Stories of his rotten, drunken father who had left the family and gone back to Alabama, never to return or to send support, never to send a card on his son's birthday, or any other day for that matter.

"Good riddance," he would often hear his mother and grandmother say. They said it was best this way. He remembered he did not like them to say such things, yet he never told them his feelings. And he always hoped his father would return to see him some day. He never did.

He remembered when he was five years old, beginning his new life at the immense Von Humboldt Elementary School on Chicago's west side. There he found an environment that was opposite of that provided by his mother and grandmother.

He absorbed the new ideas and concepts, the words and the numbers, the different ways to function and to think. He loved it all.

By the time he reached sixth grade he was an excellent student and his behavior was generally good at school and in the community. But in the summer before he began sixth grade he became a friend with some older boys in their early teens who had just joined a gang called the Vice Lords.

The eleven-year-old was a big, mature kid for his age and strong, too. More importantly, and even more influential, was his marvelous intellect and his verbal skills in communicating his thoughts and ideas and his stories. Those highly entertaining stories, which were made up and not true in any sense, were what established his initial reputation with his older friends, and soon afterwards, with the leaders of the gang.

As he lay in his bed trying to sleep, he remembered his decision to join the gang. It really was his decision. He had wanted to join. Of course, under the circumstances, if he had not wanted to join, he knew trouble would have caught up with him very fast and very hard. But he loved their acceptance of him as someone of worth and value. There was some hierarchy to the gang and some order and discipline that made sense. Most of all there was a feeling of belonging, almost like being part of a family that cared about you and was loyal to you and would never leave you. No, he remembered the day he became a member of the Vice Lords was the happiest and proudest day of his young life.

His teachers in his first six years of school had generally been good ones. They were conscientious and had reasonable control of their classrooms in terms of discipline and the effectiveness of their teaching.

But within fifteen minutes of the first day of sixth grade he knew he had a loser. Within an hour of the first day discipline had broken down, never to return. For two weeks bedlam and chaos reigned. At first he tried to behave himself, for it was not in his nature to enjoy disorder. But gradually, because it was useless to do anything else, he worked himself into the role of class leader of teacher torment and again found he enjoyed being the center of attention, where everyone followed his lead. It was a glorious two weeks, even though in the quietness of his room at home he felt some shame in what he was doing.

On Monday morning of the third week of school the principal and assistant principal greeted the class as it was led into the room by the obviously distraught teacher. His name and two others were called out and told to wait in the hallway and be quiet about it, too. Even though the classroom door was shut, he heard the stern lecture, the unveiled threats of punishment of what could be expected if further chaos continued. He knew it would continue for numerous reasons, one of which was that the three boys they had pulled from the class were the wrong choices.

Marched to the principal's office, they were severely lectured, with their records so noted, and then taken to a classroom taught by a teacher by the name of Mr. Ray. The other two boys groaned when they heard who was to be their new teacher. But for a reason he could not quite identify, he felt relief and a sense of renewed purpose, a new beginning, that would take him out of the meanness arena into which his life had found itself.

After a hurried conference the assistant principal left the boys standing at the teacher's desk. He looked at them for a moment, this not-so-large man with glasses, and then with a soft voice told each of them where to sit. The class was silent, going about their work, with an occasional glance at the newcomers.

One by one he talked to them quietly as they came up and sat in the chair next to his desk. And when each returned to his seat there was not the slightest thought in any of their minds that they would do anything but follow the rules of the room and of Mr. Ray. There was no question who ruled there.

Sixth grade became a good year for there was order and civility in the confines of his classroom. His leadership and academic achievements were strong and positive and he felt a real sense of worth while inside the walls of Von Humboldt.

But outside those walls his conduct and his values were slowly beginning to deteriorate as the power of the Vice Lords bent its will in his life. Stealing from stores on Division Street and North Avenue, stealing cars for parts and for joy rides, fighting other gangs, were all part of the changing scene of his young life, as he moved rapidly to that of a "gang banger".

In his freshman year of high school, the gang began to buy drugs to sell to those who were hooked in their neighborhood. Gradually their market widened as others in the city and suburbs rolled to the right corner for their share, and the gangs fledgling business of drug selling in just a few years became a huge enterprise of death and destruction and misery.

But strangely enough, this thief, this fighter, this dealer of death, who was rising to high positions of leadership within the Vice Lords and becoming the best of the gang bangers, never missed a day of school from his first day of kindergarten at Von Humboldt to the day he graduated from Orr High School thirteen years later.

He had somehow managed to live two lives and no one had caught him at it. His grades were the very best and luckily no one had discovered that, either. There were many close calls with the police, but each time he was picked up he was released for one reason or another. They were always impressed by his ability to communicate intelligently with them and in a way they seemed to enjoy. Somehow they always believed his lies and released him.

But in the summer after his high school graduation, his luck ran out and his life fell apart. On a hot July night he was walking with four other Vice Lords along Division Street to meet a regular customer, a guy from the suburbs, who bought big and often. They were all carrying some of the drugs, which they knew was foolish, but it was a last minute request and no time to set up the regular delivery procedure. Besides, they knew they were invincible. They were the Vice Lords!

A car moved slowly behind them. They were alert to danger but their brazen carelessness made it easy, too easy. The car pulled even with them and for a single moment they realized the reality of what was going to happen. They reached for their guns, but the bullets were already hitting them, tearing their flesh and organs and breaking their bones.

Four of them died within a minute as they lay writhing on the bloody sidewalk. The gang banger's leg bone was shattered, and a bullet had entered his lung, another his stomach. He lay gasping for breath. He knew he was dying. He was afraid, very afraid. No one approached for they too were afraid. Finally, in the distance, through his fear and suffering, he heard sirens and the thought that plunged though his mind was, "Why am I here like this? Why am I here?"

He barely survived the three bullets, but he did, thanks to a strong body and good doctoring, and, as he thought about it in the years that followed, God's grace and mercy. For his efforts he received a limp in his walk for the rest of his life, an empty space where a lung used to be, Less stomach than he started the day with, and five years in prison.

So long ago it seemed, in both time and the way his life had moved and changed. He thought of the weeks of struggle and pain in the hospital, before he went to court and then to prison. He remembered how he had slipped in and out of consciousness those first few days at Cook County Hospital.

He remembered the jail chaplain, Steve Thompson, talking, praying actually, next to his ear, saying his name and the name, "Jesus," over and over. He remembered the peace he felt when he heard his voice. It had felt good. It was the only thing that had been good since the bullets flew into his body and nearly destroyed him on that horrible July night. Also, it was the only time anyone had ever prayed for him in his entire life.

Prison was claustrophobic. His mind and spirit suffocated from his loss of freedom, the indignities the inmates put each other through, the fear of violence, and the abuse. It took months to adjust to the horrible reality that prison was to be his home for up to five years.

Eventually, what saved him was the educational system in the prison and its library. Every minute he could find available he spent reading. He read the classics, as well as contemporary literature. He read biographies of great men and women and the historical times in which they lived. Philosophy, law, medical, and political books were hoarded into his mind. For three years he was obsessed with learning. It pleased him when he found he had the ability to understand and apply in his thinking these ideas to which he was being exposed.

In the fourth year of his imprisonment he found he was reading mostly books of law and it was in that year he be-

WHO IS GOING TO HEAVEN?

gan to realize that perhaps law was the field of study he would attempt when he gained his freedom. If they would let him. The shadow of a felon was long and dark.

He had never been religious or had any interest in religion of any flavor or variety. It was not that he was an atheist. He supposed there might be a God. It was not that he was antagonistic against religion. It was fine for those who wanted it. "Live and let live" was his motto, as far as religion was concerned. He thought of himself as neutral in that area and was rather proud of that tolerant position.

But for all the reading he had done in his lifetime, he had never read the Bible, or even thought of it for that matter. There was no particular reason he had never read it. He just never had.

In the very early hours just before dawn, he realized he had only dozed a few times during the night. Sleep and rest were escaping him, it seemed. He thought about another night long ago in a prison cell where he found himself sleeping only for a short time, then abruptly waking, sweating, and shaking with violent tremors at the shock of what he was dreaming. It had happened not once, but five times during that horrible night, the most vivid, the most terrifying dreams he had ever experienced.

At the beginning of each dream he had died violent, horrible deaths, each one different and each one worse than the one before. After each of his deaths he was taken and thrown into a hole in the ground and covered with earth. But in his dream he knew that he was still alive and even as he cried out to his tormenters, and knew they could not hear him, he suffocated and died a second time there in the grave.

But again he awoke in the hole and the darkness and the earth pressed down upon him, so even when he tried to cry out he could not. After each time that seemed to last forever the grave opened and he fell tumbling over and over again through blazing fires until he reached what he knew without doubt was the place called hell.

The stench overwhelmed him, even in his dream. It was not the stench of smell, but the stench of evil that came to him in each of his dreams. This horrible display of evil always met him first, and then, different in each dream were the terrible feelings that followed. The feeling of pain—physical pain was there, yes, but even more so was the excruciating pain of hopelessness—and the loneliness, the knowledge you would never talk or see anyone again, ever. The darkness of the place was maddening. No light. No light. In the last dream the feeling of regret was so strong that he heard himself cry out to God. But God was not there. God could not be there. When he understood this, regret became his main torturer, never receding, always present, always ready to mock him. At the end of each dream came the realization that righteousness could no longer exist, that goodness was gone forever, that evil was permanent, never to leave him.

At the end of the fifth dream he jumped out of his bunk and stood shaking in horror by the cell door, afraid he might go to sleep again and dream. As he stood in the dim light of the cell block he thought about his life, not his worldly life, for he knew he would never return to the gang and drugs and crime again. That part of his life was over, he hoped.

But what of his soul, his eternal destiny? What of God? What did God want from him? Would God even want him?

There was, however, one thing of which he was certain. There was a place he knew as hell that he never wanted to be near again. He had been there.

The cell block was quiet except for some snores and moans and a few men talking to themselves or someone in their sleep. The Vice Lord went to his bunk, quietly, so he would not disturb his cell mate. He sat down on it and began to pray. Not with prayer words of a preacher or bishop, but honest, blunt words of the street.

He asked God for help, to know what to pray. But mostly he begged God. He begged God to keep him out of hell, even though he knew he probably deserved it. He pleaded with God to tell him what he had to do to stay out of that horrible place he had lived in his dreams. He would do anything, he said, anything. And then after a long time of pleading he became silent and waited. And listened.

For what, he had no idea. He really did not expect a voice or writing on a wall. But he did expect something. So he waited, occasionally encouraging God to do something to let him know his fate, but mostly there was silence in his waiting, listening, expecting.

He could not exactly pinpoint or describe the moment of beginning, but slowly and quietly ideas and pieces of understanding began to probe his mind and thinking. The first thought that began to spread through his consciousness was that God loved him, loved him totally and without conditions. The realization of this made his face grow hot and then without warning tears flooded his eyes. He dropped to his knees, weeping silently at the thought of being loved by the great God of heaven and earth.

He then began to think about his life, the kind of person he had become, the things in his life that were wrong. And as he thought on these things, it became very clear to him why he felt separated from God. Even as a nonreligious man he now knew what it was that kept him from God, and in supreme danger of hell. It was what even he recognized as sin.

And so again he prayed, begging God to forgive and take away the wrong things that were in his life. He listed before God those things he could remember that needed forgiving. He told God he was truly sorry, for he knew they were sinful and evil, and he guessed that must make him sinful and evil, too.

After his dreams he wanted nothing more to do with evil. He wanted to be clean before God, not dirty like he had been. He asked God to make him clean. He asked God to allow him in heaven when he died.

Again he became silent and waited, and the Holy Spirit who had attempted to guide and teach him since his birth, brought to his heart and mind and soul a peace that was beyond the gang member's understanding. He was filled with joy, for he knew at that moment that he was free from his sin.

Yet he did not know why he was free. Of course he had heard of Jesus Christ. Who had not, unless you lived in some jungle or on top of a remote mountain? As a matter of fact, he often mentioned the name of Jesus Christ numerous times throughout each and every day. Certainly he knew him as a religious figure who was said to have died on a cross. He even knew to one degree or another the various doctrines of the Christian faith. But he had never connected everything together into God's plan of salvation for mankind and for himself. And no one had ever been able to tell him of this singular way to find God, and if someone had, he probably would not have been ready to respond.

But this night the Holy Spirit had come to him with great might and power, and he had responded to the Spirit's call. He did not know, nor did he understand, Jesus Christ's role in his salvation. But even without this knowledge or understanding that it was Jesus who had paid the debt for his sins through his death on the cross, the gang banger's life had been transformed and God had received him into his kingdom.

An older man now, the old Vice Lord, he had given up trying to sleep. He remembered back to that moment when peace had come to his life in that prison cell so long ago. It had happened as dawn broke and the first of the sun's rays had come into the windows of his cell block. It was the most wonderful moment of his life and he would treasure it forever.

He thought of all the things that had happened in his life since that dawn meeting with God and his soul. He had been released from prison soon afterwards, a year-and-a-half short of his five-year sentence. For this he was very grateful. He was twenty-one years old.

He had found a part-time job at a local Jewel Food Store, and lived with his mother and grandmother in the same apartment in which he grew up. He went back to school at the University of Illinois' Circle Campus for four years, where he received a degree, with majors in philosophy and economics.

The gang had wanted him back in the fold, but his glib tongue was able to persuade their leaders they were better off without him. His wounds, prison time, and the fact that he did not reject them, but wanted to keep them as his friends, played a large part in them allowing him to live and work in the gang's territory.

Soon after leaving prison he bought a Bible and started reading. It was then he came to understand what his relationship to Jesus Christ really was and what Jesus had done for him on the cross. Not only had Jesus been his savior, but now he had become his personal savior, whom he came to know and love more fully as he prayed and read the Bible.

He knew there had to be others around him who believed in God and Jesus and read the Bible. He felt a strong need in his life to meet these people, whoever they were. He remembered there was an organization on North Avenue that was for kids in the neighborhood. He had never been there before, although he had walked by it many times. So he crossed North Avenue late one afternoon before going to work and entered the doors of Inner City Impact.

It was there that he met Bill Dillon, who for the next two years helped the ex-Vice Lord grow in his spiritual life. In turn, he helped kids in the neighborhood stay away from the darkness in which he had found himself, the darkness that had nearly destroyed him.

Toward the end of his time at the university he had met another man who was to have a great influence in his life. Gordon McLean worked with gangs in Chicago. For several years they worked together with Chicago street gangs and gradually there was a lessening of gang conflicts and gang activities in some Chicago neighborhoods.

Many of the gang members became followers of Jesus Christ and, like the ex-Vice Lord, changed their approach to life and found the peace and purpose by which they could live their lives.

After his graduation from the University of Illinois, the former gang banger was accepted at John Marshall Law School in Chicago. A number of people had helped him overcome the obstacle of being a felon and having served time. And a great many people were praying that he would be accepted. He was exuberant when he heard he would be going, and from the very beginning, loved the challenge and competition he found there.

During his first year of law school he began to be involved with the local Democratic Party, helping with campaigning, mostly posting and handing out literature, but on several occasions giving speeches to small groups for the local candidate for the Illinois state legislature. It was his superb storytelling ability and delivery style that eventually brought him to the attention of the Democratic leadership toward the end of his last year in law school. Even though it was highly unusual, he was handpicked by the powerful mayor of Chicago to run for election in the place of an old, established Chicago alderman who had died.

The former Vice Lord thought back on those fantastic days and the years that followed. He had, of course, won the aldermanic election. Chicago politics in those days was pretty well controlled by the mayor and the party. It was the first of many election victories that would follow in the years and decades ahead for the young politician.

Each new victory and responsibility increased his experience, his knowledge, and his wisdom as he dealt with legislative and executive problems and decisions. His ability to relate with other people was superb. He came across both publicly and privately as a good and godly man, whose primary interests were the people he served and the country he had grown to love so much.

Since that early morning decision in his prison cell, the crowning day of his life, he had never wavered in his love and devotion to his Lord and savior. So as dawn finally lightened the eastern sky, he prayed to the God of the universe and the God of his life to bless him and this day that was before him. Then he rose from his bed and made himself ready. They came for him soon afterwards and led him away.

It was noon on a cold, clear winter morning when he finally stood before a waiting world and placed his left hand on his first Bible, opened to the third chapter of the Apostle John. Then he raised his right hand and looked into the eyes of the robed man who stood in front of him.

"I, gang banger, do solemnly swear," said the robed man.
"I, gang banger, do solemnly swear," the gang banger repeated.
"That I will faithfully execute the office of President of the United States."
"That I will faithfully execute the office of President of the United States."
"And I will to the best of my ability,"
"And I will to the best of my ability,"
"Preserve, protect, and defend the Constitution of the United States"
"Preserve, protect, and defend the Constitution of the United States"
"So help me God."
"So help me God."

# EIGHT

## THE MAINLINER

In America, during the first half of the twentieth century, most Protestant denominations as well as the Roman Catholic Church prospered, as church membership and attendance increased. Along with this growth was the tendency of church parishioners to maintain and follow the religious values and standards established by their church.

But somewhere in the middle of the century—the timing depending on the church group and sometimes on which faction within the church group—the trend was reversed with large segments of the American population eventually becoming less attentive to their church and to the values for which they had stood.

This does not necessarily mean people became less religious or spiritual, but they did become disinterested in many of the mainline churches to the point of dropping out of active worship and service within the church structure.

Why did this occur? The primary reason appears to be that many of these churches simply became irrelevant in the task of fulfilling the needs of their congregations. This seems particularly true in the most important need of all: teaching the way that God has provided for us to have eternal life.

They lived in a typical small, Midwest city, this wife and husband of thirty some years of marriage. Their three children were grown and had families scattered throughout the country. She owned an accounting business and operated it out of a strip shopping center near her home. They had numerous friends, very sufficient income, and generally enjoyed life, which centered around friends, neighborhood, and church activities, as well as vacationing several times a year, though not during tax season.

She and her husband belonged to a church group that had been established generations ago, and if any church qualified as a mainline church, it was theirs. The mainliner's church might have been part of almost any established and traditional Christian denomination or faith. It could have been Methodist, Baptist, Roman Catholic, Lutheran, Presbyterian, Christian Reform, Congregational, or one of many others that existed in America as the twentieth century finished its course.

It is really not important. With certain exceptions, most mainline Christian churches believe basically the same doctrines. However, style, method of worship, and emphasis placed on these doctrines, may vary substantially. Very often, there are greater differences found within a denomination or faith than between these church groups in terms of how they "work out" their faith.

The mainliner enjoyed going to church on Sunday morning. She loved the hymns and anthems that were song by the choir and the congregation. The quiet, yet powerful, liturgy of the scriptures, the sacred prayers, the use of strong and often dramatic words, with their deep symbolic meanings, always moved her conscientious thoughts toward God.

She always felt good for being there. She felt she had a connection to God when surrounded by the symbols, the images, the wonderful musical and spoken sounds radiating throughout the beautiful room that was her own holy sanctuary. It was the place she could feel God's presence, the place she could feel safe in today's harsh world, and because of these good feelings, perhaps safe in the world to come when she would leave this one in death.

But sadly, the feeling of security and safety seemed to dissipate on Monday morning, or Tuesday, or sometime later in the week. She thought of these fluctuating feelings often and wished they could be stable and permanent in her life. She hated being so unsure about her relationship with God. At times she felt it was a correct relationship and at other times she had no idea how she stood with God. And as she grew older she had become more and more fearful of the time she would die.

Even though she had listened to hundreds of sermons over the years, and tried to listen carefully for the one important answer to her secret fear, the answer never reached her ears, or if it did, there was no understanding.

Her pastor was a good man. He loved his congregation and worked long hard hours to serve and minister to them. He believed in the doctrines that Christians all over the world believe. Not only did he believe them to be true and reliable, but he had a strong desire to teach these truths to his congregation.

His excellent ability to use words effectively in communicating God's Word was experienced by all who came into the presence of his preaching. He was quite eloquent. If he had a weakness—which in fact he did—it was his pride in his speaking ability. It was also his downfall as a minister of the gospel of Christ.

For though everything he taught in his preaching was truth, there was a part of the gospel that was not taught, or if taught, preached in such a way that it was difficult for his congregation to grasp or understand its truth or meaning.

The doctrines and concepts of God's love and mercy were well taught. However, God's judgment, sin, and God's hatred of sin were swallowed up with easy-to-hear symbolism and double-meaning words. The teaching of heaven and angels were gladly taught and gladly received by his congregation. Hell, Satan, and his demons were strangely missing from his preaching repertoire.

The manger story was the top preaching event of the year, with Jesus' death on the cross a somewhat distant second. The resurrection was mentioned symbolically for at least one Sunday. The Second Coming of Jesus Christ? Well, no.

And so, for all her minister's highly respected teaching over the years, the mainliner and a huge number of her fellow parishioners never really heard the complete gospel of Christ, and how it could save them for eternity in heaven. And sadly, if the minister had somehow found this to be true in his preaching, it is difficult to know what he could do about it, so great was his pride.

Right on schedule it came, the mainliner's fifty-fifth birthday, a day usually filled with happy memories of celebration with family and friends. Instead it became a sad day, perhaps the saddest day of her life, when she received a phone call from her father with the news that her mother had suddenly died.

The arrangements for the wake, the funeral, the graveside service, all had become a blur in her mind. As she found herself in the bedroom of her home the day of her mother's burial, she asked herself if she had really mourned for her mother. She was not sure, really. How could one tell if mourning occurred? Perhaps she would feel it later, whatever that feeling might be. Now her thoughts centered around herself, her own life, and her own eventual death. After all, she was in the next generation to go. She also realized that a person's life could end at any time and not wait for the three score and ten, or twenty, and more often now, with modern medicine and health care, three score and thirty years, or longer.

All her life she had tried to be a good person, really a good person, not a fake or a hypocrite. And in human terms, even though she would never even think it herself, she was that good person, probably one of the nicest people ever to exist on this planet.

Why then did she have this uncertainty about God and her relationship to him? Why was she so worried, actually terrified, about this business of dying?

She had never prayed much, except when reading printed prayers, or for grace at meals, or occasional short petition prays for people for whom she promised to pray. But tonight she prayed intensely, asking—begging would be more like it—for God to show her how she could have the assurance when the time of her death came that she would be welcome in heaven.

As she prayed, the Holy Spirit began teaching her about sin, and into her mind and heart came the understanding that God hated sin and that sin was very repugnant to him. The Spirit taught her that in God's presence and in his heaven there is no sin, no place for sin. Even the smallest "innocent" sin could not exist in the holy presence of the living God.

Slowly into her mind, heart, and soul came the realization, the conviction that she was sinful, not only because of her conduct through her thoughts and deeds, but her very nature, her inner self, her psyche makeup, bore the weight of sin, the crushing, condemning weight of sin. And as this understanding permeated her soul, like millions before her over the centuries, she cried out to God for her sins to be forgiven, to be removed from her soul, to no longer be a woman of sin, but rather to be a woman clean before God.

She remembered words from an old hymn she used to sing as a young girl.

Lord Jesus, I long to be perfectly whole;
I want you forever to live in my soul.
Now wash me and I will be whiter than snow.

That became her prayer, that she be made clean and pure like a new fallen snow. And so, sometime during this time of prayer of confession, of turning from her sin, she was born into the family of God.

She may not have recognized what had actually happened, but she knew her mind and spirit were no longer fearful. She had a quiet peace that brought her tumult to an end. And before she slept that night she thanked God for hearing and answering her prayers, for giving her his blessing of peace and assurance. In the days that followed she shared with her pastor what had happened in her life and he said he was happy for her, but she felt he did not understand what had really happened. His sermons continued as before, eloquent and effective, except in that most important area of a preacher's preaching.

She began to read and study a family Bible, strangely enough, for the first time in a mode that could be called searching. And though she had heard all of her life of Jesus Christ and the doctrines and events that surrounded his life, she had never understood what he personally did for her when he died on the cross. Now she understood and rejoiced.

In the following months she met other Christian believers who gave her additional strength for her walk with God. She became a member of a Bible study group and even managed to persuade her husband to join her from time to time.

She again went to her pastor and shared with him the enthusiasm she had for her new spiritual life, and he in turn seemed very supportive of the changes that were occurring in her life. However, when she, with trepidation and a little fear, had asked him why he did not share these crucial truths of the gospel with their congregation, she was met with complete silence for several moments.

He then responded by saying there were many ways to share the gospel of Christ and he needed to share it on a less emotional level, one that would preserve its dignity and still share its good news. He felt the gospel would speak for itself if preached in a way that would appeal to all people and not turn them off to the word of God.

After a time of listening, nor refuting his words and arguing her own thoughts, she left his office and the church that cool, autumn afternoon, and after a number of days of prayer and thinking, decided she must find a different church in which to worship and serve. It was a difficult task, leaving the church of her lifetime, but she felt strongly that it was the right choice for her.

Over the years her faith grew and her relationship with her Lord was strengthened as she lived her life so it would be pleasing to him. And before she died at a very old age she found herself the spiritual matriarch and example to dozens of grandchildren and great-grandchildren, along with their spouses and other extended family.

God had richly blessed her on earth and yet that blessing was only the beginning of her eternal reward that would never end.

Strangely enough, about two years after she had left her first church, she heard of changes occurring there. Great increases in church attendance, revitalized social outreach programs to the community, Bible study groups dramatically increasing in number, and most amazing of all, spiritual revival within the church, with scores of people becoming Christian believers.

One Sunday morning she squeezed into a back row of the crowded sanctuary of her old church and experienced a worship service that utterly amazed her. The brilliant and eloquent preaching still rang through the room, but its content was the powerful message of a saving Christ.

As her old preacher walked to the back of the sanctuary after the service to greet his congregation, he stopped at the row in which she was seated, stood looking at her for a moment, and with a tear forming on his cheek, took her hand, and whispered, "Thank you."

# NINE

## THE CHURCHMAN

### Prayers for America

America! America! God mend their every flaw.
"America the Beautiful"

Long may our land be bright with freedom's holy light;
Protect us by thy might, great God, our King.
"My Country, 'Tis of Thee"

America, the greatest country in the world, the experiment in democracy, the land of the free, the home of the brave, the place in which most people of the world would love to live, the "melting pot of the world."

Now that's a great saying, but not true now and probably never has been. We the people may coordinate our goals and ideas occasionally, but we are certainly not a melting pot, in language, religion, politics, or our lifestyles. And the list can go on and on.

Land of the free? Yes, we are! All right, not totally, for we do not choose to be totally free. And would not enjoy it anyway. Anarchy and all that stuff. Bad for the kids!

How free should we be? Ask a hundred people and hear a hundred different thoughts. We melt together all right, if I own the mold and I do the pouring! I'm right. That's it. No question about it! Only strong opinions need apply, here in America!

Many things make America great. One is our freedom to think, speak, and do what we want to think, say, and do, within certain limits. Hopefully these limits will be determined and enforced by the laws our government, which has been guided even more hopefully, by the laws of God.

But these two forces, these two immense powers in our lives—the laws of government and of God—as we well know, are not always compatible. And when there is conflict between the two, Americans tend to choose the side that they will support, based on a multitude of reasons, from the very worst possible motives to the very best.

Not only are there conflicts between the laws of God and the laws of Caesar in this American Republic, but as Americans determine which side of an issue they are on, immense struggles can come into play as these laws are voted into our legal system, and interpreted and supported, or not supported, by the citizens. Not only do struggles and fighting occur between these power groups of Americans, but factions and divisions often occur within their own organizations as they go at it against each other for perhaps lesser or greater evils then they find themselves facing from the outside.

The Christian church in America often finds itself in great turmoil as it determines, and then attempts to carry out, its agendas in the free society in which we live. And what an array of controversial subjects from which to operate these agendas! Abortion, homosexuality, prayer in public schools, the unwholesomeness of television, creationism and evolution, electing the "right" public officials, fighting over doctrine and procedures, and doing it all in public. And these are only some of the most prominent of all the controversies one might be exposed to here in America.

The involvement of churches, individuals, and parachurch organizations in these agendas or movements range from an almost radical proactive philosophy to a laissez faire, let's not get too involved attitude. They may be single individuals, small churches or immense national organizations with millions of followers. The one thing all these individuals and organizations seem to have in common is that they know they are right and the other side is wrong—usually totally wrong! And so the battle rages on and on and on.

## The Churchman

His family was a typical American family. At least it would have been back in the 1950's and 1960's. In today's world his family and their lifestyle would be far from typical of what we now find in American society. Things have changed in the last forty or fifty years. Oh, how they have changed!

They lived in a suburb of a middle-sized city in the state of Kansas. He was a manufacturer's representative for a farm implement company and traveled throughout a three-state area, occasionally staying overnight for his work. His wife was a housewife and their four children ranged in age from six to fourteen.

They rarely missed a Sunday of going to church. His church had a tradition of "preaching the Bible" and "telling it like it is." It was in the forefront of fighting for family values in their community, state, and country. He was proud to be a member of such a church.

Prior to 1975, he and his wife had not attended church, nor had they had a tradition of being involved in a church as they grew up. Then one spring evening the young pastor of a church that had just started a few months earlier in their neighborhood knocked on their door and asked if he might talk to them for a moment or two. They invited him in and two hours and numerous cups of coffee later they had become good friends and dedicated to the idea of being involved with this dynamic young leader in building a church that loved God, America, and the family, which they thought appropriate since their first baby was due in five months.

Over the years the church grew steadily in membership and attendance. It was in a growing area, with many young families moving in. The pastor was an excellent speaker and a fine administrator, and he certainly had the ability to lead people. Part of this ability was the appealing message he preached, that of loving God, loving one's country, and stressing the right family values for families in his church, as well as for their community and nation.

As the years passed through the 1980's and 1990's and into the 2000's, the churchman's church took on stronger and more vocal roles in its involvement with agendas that focused on the buzzword and concept of "family values." The emphasis for expanding the church family by reaching out to those in the neighborhoods and new subdivisions growing up around the church gradually was pushed aside by an emphasis and dedication to politicking, protesting, and pressuring.

The church had been caught up in the fight over the fast-moving social and cultural changes that were occurring in America, the country they loved and wanted to protect.

Fighting against abortion at the local level, as well as at the state and national levels, was by far the most emotional issue, and certainly the agenda that took the most time, money, and energy of the church and its people. It came first. Nothing else was a close second. Abortion clinics and hospitals, as well as homes of abortion doctors, were picketed. The pastor delivered numerous sermons on the subject. Large amounts of money were spent on antiabortion literature and its distribution. The movement had become an all out battle. And heaven help the candidate for local, state, or national office who was not pro-life! It was a cause for which a person could give his entire life and resources to fight, so horrible was this crime against God and humanity.

Creeping into a position to further threaten family values in America was the homosexual agenda. Not content to live and let live—which until recently our country's laws were not willing to do for them—the gays were fighting for rights that many in the country felt were not due them as a separate entity in our society. This was another subject for the pulpit on Sunday, for people to talk about, get angry over, do a little bit of mocking and ridiculing, and even perhaps a small amount of hating. And it came from both sides of the issue, this emotional turmoil that was pitting human beings against each other.

There has always been controversy existing within the realm of American public education. The subject of the controversy depends on the decade or century one is talking about. During the last part of the twentieth century there have been many things happening in the public schools that seem to ignore God and his laws.

God, in most cases, seems to be a second-class citizen in his own world, if he is even a citizen at all. And if he comes to school he had better be quiet! No, "I created the world" kind of foolishness.

And certainly no attempt to compete with the "completely proven, infallible theory" of evolution will be tolerated. No new ideas, if you don't mind. Creationism? Oh, please, not that.

And if you really must pray, do it with your eyes open so it's not so obvious. And silently. Just listen to that little Buddhist kid two rows over muttering to himself.

Sarcasm, a little ridicule, you say? I suppose, and it's just what will be preached against a little later in the story. But it felt so good!

Then there is the demon-infested TV industry. Little good comes out of the land of American television. Only if you are extremely careful can you view programming of any redemptive value such as football, baseball, or basketball. What? Who is that yelling and screaming? Well, alright then, would the History and Discovery channels suit you? Maybe Meet the Press or Mr. Rogers Neighborhood?

Actually, American television has an immense amount of excellent programming. But the right buttons do have to get pushed. No one is being forced to watch the goofy sitcoms, soaps, talk shows, and so on.

So these were the "anti," the "against," and the "ungodly" issues that consumed the church's time, energies, and resources, and as a result threatened the integrity of the gospel of Jesus Christ in the society in which this church lived and to which it was to minister.

Alas, there were no Democrats attending the churchman's church. Well, there might have been a few who inherited the party from their fathers, but they were closet Democrats and kept their mouths shut, or maybe lied a little bit when push came to shove. On one hand, every right winger in America knows that a right-wing Republican is incapable of making a mistake or coming up with a wrong decision, whereas a liberal Democrat has no capacity whatsoever of doing anything right. On the other hand, the liberal knows for certain that nothing good has ever come from a right-wing anything, And nothing ever will. Ever!

Labels are wonderful. It's a method by which we all can know who and what we stand for, and for whom we stand against, who our friends are, and who our enemies are. It's very comfortable that way!

Over the years the churchman and his wife were involved in the proactive movement of the church as it fought against the "abortion is okay" philosophy that was encroaching into their city and the American society. Often you could see one or both on the picket line in front of one of several small hospitals or clinics that provided abortions in their city. They went to prayer vigils, wrote letters to government officials, and read books and other literature about this scourge of the twentieth century.

To a lesser extent was his involvement in the fight to prevent the placement of teachers with open alternative lifestyles in the public school classrooms. He attended and spoke up at school board meeting, wrote letters to the editors of the local newspapers, and gave his views to anyone who cared to listen—and to some who did not.

Although not involved directly with the issues of evolution and creationism, or prayer in the schools, the churchman spent a great deal of time and energy talking about these areas of conflict and disagreement.

During the years since the pastor first called at their home on that beautiful spring evening, the churchman had two major agendas in his church life. The first was to do everything he could to build his church into a thriving center for people in the community to come and hear about God and to raise their families with strong Biblical principles as their guide.

There was also a common thread he made sure was always present in the philosophy and policies of his church. It was that America, their beloved country, was to be valued, respected, and loved as the greatest nation on earth.

Immense amounts of time, energy, and emotional resources went into this highly successful endeavor, and from this success he found a great deal of inner satisfaction. As the scene shifted in his church from community outreach to social activism, the churchman never missed a beat, as he poured his life into this new arena of activity. And again, the common force motivating him was that America, his beloved country, and the society within its framework, needed to be defended against the forces that were trying to destroy her, or at least change her traditional values.

If anyone had asked if the churchman was a Christian, a believer, a part of God's family, born again, or whatever word or words might describe a true relationship with God, the answer would have been an unqualified yes. By honest human standards he was a good man, and he was certainly zealous for working and giving himself to what everyone considered godly pursuits. There were not too many things for which you could fault the churchman. Well, maybe he did talk too much, but he was a salesman after all, so that was to be expected. Over all, though, he was a likable man, a good man. And if he was quite honest about it, that is how he would view himself. Which he did.

He was coming home from a long day of calls in an adjoining state that mid-November evening. The weather had turned surprisingly bad about thirty miles from home and he was driving on a two-lane highway, a shortcut he often used. It had started to snow and slick spots were forming on the road, causing him to slow his speed.

He saw the deer just as it bounded across the road in front of him. Actually, it did not quite make it across the road, but decided to stop in the center of his lane and admire the bright lights coming toward him. His horn and brakes operated as one, but the deer was thoroughly enjoying his view and stayed put. It was the last thing the deer saw as the skidding car struck it at fifty miles per hour.

Headlights went out, antlers shattered the windshield, and the car went into a swirling spin down the road for a hundred yards until it plunged off a ten-foot slope, turned over twice, rolled upright for a while, and crashed rather gently into several oak trees growing in the small valley below the road.

Then there was silence and darkness. He sat stunned, still in the front seat with seat belts still around him and an air bag lying limp in his lap. He very carefully moved his arms and legs, shifted his weight around in his seat, and to his amazement felt no pain. He tried breathing in deep breaths of air and found he could, again, with no pain. He was OK! He made it!

He smiled to himself, unsnapped the safety belt and attempted to open his door. It would not budge. Neither would the passenger door he could barely reach. Then the realization came to him. He could not move out of his seating position very far at all. He could not get out!

The roof was caved in and the seats were pushed up to the front. The best he could do was lay partially down on the front seat. Then it started to get cold. His heavy topcoat and even his suit coat were on the back seat. No matter how hard he tried he could not reach either of them. He was becoming thoroughly frightened. Snow started falling heavier and blew into the car and drifted all over him. He began shivering, unable to stop. He yelled but the wind drowned out his voice before it reached the highway. He was being covered with snow and he was terribly cold. It was then he knew he was going to die.

And that thought terrified him, for it was not just the thought of leaving his good life, his family, the years he would normally have left to live, but the terrible realization he was not ready to die, not ready to meet God. How could that be, he thought. All I have done for the church, for other people, for God. But even with those thoughts, deep down in his heart and soul, he really knew the answer.

He was a man of sin. It was part of him. He felt its horrendous weight now, this unbearable weight of sin on his soul. He always had known it was there, but had pushed the truth away, pushed the Holy Spirit away time after time, and replaced the truth with activity and good works. But now as death was approaching, all the good things he had done did not seem to matter, did not count for anything.

It was then he called out to God in a loud voice, asking that the sin in his life be forgiven, that God would have mercy on him, a sinner. His mind began to process the truths he had learned in church about Jesus Christ, his dying for him on the cross, the need to repent and turn from sin, and God's forgiveness, his wonderful forgiveness. And strangely, for the first time in his thinking and in his life, it all fit together.

And in the freezing cold that was quickly numbing his body, the warmth of forgiveness came to him and he knew he had been born again into eternal life. With tears falling from his eyes, he gave thanks to the God he was certain to see very soon. In the pitch darkness and eerie stillness of the winter night he waited for death to enter his life.

His mind was becoming a blur. But he was no longer as cold as he had been. For that he was thankful. He was almost ready for sleep, he thought. Yes, that's what he wanted now, more than anything, peaceful sleep, comfortable rest. His eyes closed.

And then, vaguely, from the deep recesses of his mind he heard voices and footsteps, saw lights fluttering in the darkness, heard his car being torn open, felt himself being lifted out of his comfort zone and laid flat on the snowy cold ground, heard voices say, "Bad shape." "May not make it." "It'll be close."

In the warmth of the car he fell back asleep as it sped down the highway in the darkness of the wintry night.

They took him to the first medical facility they came to, a small private hospital on the edge of town, where for two hours a doctor and medical team worked on him in a valiant effort to help him live. His wife was called and she and the children were there before he woke up, still in very rough shape, with two to three toes that appeared likely to be lost to frostbite. After the churchman's tearful reunion with his family, the doctor suggested that, since the churchman seemed out of danger of dying, the family go home so the patient could rest. The doctor assured them that the churchman would be better when they returned the next morning.

Early the next morning, the doctor who had treated him, checked the churchman and questioned him about the accident and how he was rescued. The churchman shared how the accident occurred, but he had no answer to how he was found when it was so dark and his car was so far off the road. He also shared with the doctor his experience with God as he sat trapped in his car, waiting to die while the blowing snow slowly covered his body. The doctor listened politely, but the churchman could tell he thought such an experience to be normal under the circumstances and not to have a great deal of value.

As the doctor was about to leave, there was a knock at the door and one of the men who had rescued him the night before asked if he could talk to him for a moment. After thanking him profusely, the churchman asked, "It was so dark last night and I knew my car could not be seen from the road, how did you find me?"

"How did we find you?" the man almost shouted. "Why there were lights flashing all around in that little valley. When we stopped we saw at least a dozen men walking around out there with powerful flashlights. By the time we got out of our car and down into the ravine, they had disappeared. I could hardly wait to ask you about them this morning. Who were they?"

There was silence for several moments as the rescuer and the doctor stared at the churchman. Finally, he answered slowly, "I saw no men, no lights. You are the only ones I saw out there last night."

He was to stay in the hospital several more days, and he did lose two of his toes on his left foot. Upon learning which hospital he was in, he realized he had been there before to picket, for it was a hospital that regularly performed abortions. During those days in the hospital, the young doctor who had treated him came often to check on his condition, more than medically needed, thought the churchman.

They talked initially about his physical progress, but then the doctor would turn the conversations toward the rescue, those men with flashlights, the timing of everything that saved the life of his patient. Eventually, they talked about the "religious experience," and what it meant to have ones sin forgiven by an almighty God. They talked about the sacrifice Christ made on the cross for all our sins, how he died in our place so we could have eternal life in heaven and not live an eternal death in hell. The doctor told about his own confusion and uncertainty of God's reality, and whether he really had a spiritual dimension as a part of his life.

The following day the churchman left the hospital and wondered if he would ever see the doctor again. That night before he fell asleep he thought of the disgust, and if he were honest, the near hatred, he had in the past for promoters of abortion, particularly abortion doctors. And yet, when the doctor who had treated him had said, yes, he performed abortions nearly every day, the answer saddened the churchman greatly, but no hate and anger came to his mind and heart, only sorrow and the need to lovingly show the doctor why abortion was not acceptable to God.

It was then a thought crossed the churchman's mind. What does God value the most, the life of an aborted baby, or the soul of an abortion doctor?

As he slept that night he dreamed. He dreamed of the abortion doctor in hell, screaming for mercy, but finding none. On the outskirts of hell was a crowd of people looking in at the scene, at the torment of the weeping man. And they were cheering and mocking and enjoying the sight. Happy they were, justified, pleased.

Within a week the doctor came to see the churchman. They talked of God things, eternal things, forgiveness, heaven, right things, wrong things. Of many things they spoke. And when he slept he dreamed again and the scene became heaven, he and the doctor and Jesus, talking and smiling, walking together forever.

In the months and years ahead, good changes began to emerge from the churchman's church and the city in which he lived. They were often subtle, often small, sometimes seemingly insignificant changes, but in total they began to make a difference in how abortion was perceived by the public.

The doctor began to speak to his colleagues, then to civic groups and to all people who would listen, about abortion and why it should not occur in their society. He spoke, too, of the adoption alternative. And when he spoke the words that were heard, occurred gently and lovingly, without ranker or anger or ridicule. He fought no one and tried not to make enemies, even of those who were evildoers. He knew he had been there himself, in camp with evil. And he prayed. He prayed so very much.

After a long while, one could sense a small change of attitude growing within the medical and social work community. Numerous Crisis Pregnancy Centers were started throughout the city. Public officials, including the mayor, began talking about and promoting adoption. Very slowly, it seemed to become more acceptable for unmarried mothers to allow adoption to be an alternative for their babies. It was gradually becoming known as the "correct," certainly the "smart," thing to do. The idea of unmarried mothers having a new life with which to start over, with education and a career a distinct possibility, appealed to a growing segment of women who had a child that would benefit from being adopted.

The image of families having children to love and nurture became a powerful motivation for adoption to be talked about, accepted, and made less difficult and less expensive for the adoptive family. A sizable part of the power structure of the city and state began to see the benefits of this emerging movement and added its support. There were still abortions, far too many. One is too many.

But over a period of time, within the society in which America lived and existed, there slowly occurred a transfer out of a wrong idea and a wrong philosophy, in which the acceptance of abortion had existed, and in its place came a more wholesome and godly alternative for the unborn child.

During the months following his accident the churchman began to rethink the priorities for his role in the church, and for that matter, his whole life. Through his influence, and that of other similar-minded men and women in the church, there was a shift away from the battle cry, the proactive role of fighting for social issues, to that of reaching out to the community, the lost world just outside their doors, while at the same time leading their church to become a true place of worship, Christian growth, and friendship.

The pastor who had led the church from its inception began to comprehend the drastic error that had occurred in his part of the leadership of the church. In a series of sermons he asked God's forgiveness and the congregation's forgiveness, and then he started his congregation on the road back to a true love and worship and to service to their great and living God.

The study of the Holy Scriptures replaced rhetoric and rancor. Sharing the good news of Christ replaced the politicizing and protesting. The church suddenly did not just ignore these social issues they had battled with all these years. They were still taught and proclaimed as wrong for our society, but done in a spirit of godliness and love and understanding.

The overwhelming result of this change of direction and behavior was that the Holy Spirit was allowed to take over the wasted and ruinous efforts of men and women and have the opportunity to work in the lives of people whose hearts and souls needed to be changed.

—◆—

The churchman's church could be any number of Christian churches in America today in some degree or another. It was doctrinally sound. The basic teachings of the Bible were believed and taught. The gospel message of God's salvation was proclaimed. Much of the time, however, it was wedged into the preaching and teaching of anti this and anti that.

The power of the gospel was lost because of striving against the "enemy," the man against man, the us against them syndrome that prevailed in the general attitude of the people. This, along with its lack of love and concern for those whose philosophy of life they opposed, robbed the Holy Spirit from working in the lives of the "doers of evil."

The church began to measure its spiritual progress, at least subconsciously, by the number of protests made, letters written, sermons preached, and the amount of press and TV coverage attained, good or bad. It was a sure sign of God blessing them, they thought, when they receive negative media coverage.

What they failed to understand was those very people, the "enemy" to whom they were supposed to be "salt and light," very often thought them to be unstable, unlikable, undesirable, unappealing, and a real turnoff. When God's truth and light did reach the ears of the unsaved, the Holy Spirit often found himself unable to perform his role of teacher, guide, and inspirer in their lives, because of the damage caused by people who were doctrinally sound, but who had replaced love, compassion, and understanding with ridicule, name calling, and a man-against-man philosophy.

What was not realized by most—for all the effort and work generated by the churchman's church—nothing really changed. The ungodly agendas moved steadily forward. There were occasional victories for the good guys: a positive newspaper article, a favorable court decision, or a convert to the cause. But over all, the tide of evil, of "wrongness," could not be stopped in any of the social agendas they were fighting against.

Why? The principles of human relationships as taught in the Holy Scriptures were not involved in the process. God's power was missing from the battle. With rare exception, nothing could or would change the mind of the follower of abortion rights, the homosexual, the TV station owner, the member of the school board, or the judge on the bench.

Protests would not. Debates would not. Favorable court decisions would not. The tide could be shifted a little, slowed temporarily, but not stopped permanently, and never reversed.

Love, and the godly attitudes that go with love, were not directed at doers of evil. Only ridicule, sarcasm, dislike, hate, and confrontation met them head on.

The continual battle of man against another man had prevailed as it has throughout the history of mankind. But in this battle there existed the Christian once again. And this was the shame of it, the shame God must feel for his people who enter the battle without the Holy Spirit. For the Holy Spirit was not allowed to work, to change hearts. He was eliminated from the process God had initiated to renew lives and bring people to himself.

Christians in that environment of confrontation and ill will were not salt and light, but dung and darkness to the unbeliever who so desperately needed to experience the love of Christ.

If, like the churchman and his church, we are guilty of fighting the battle in a way that the Holy Spirit is not prevailing and in control, may we turn ourselves around and away from doing an evil ourselves.

> I am the candle of the Lord,
> And truth and love more powerful than the sword!
> O fan the flame, its single gleam diffuse
> And let my spirit be the light that you can use.
> I am the candle of the Lord!
>    Joy Webb, "Candle of the Lord"

# PART 2

## THE SHEPHERD BOY

# THE SHEPHERD BOY

*Many centuries ago in the year 17 B.C.*
*There was a baby boy born*
*To a family of shepherds that lived*
*Near the town of Bethlehem,*
*In the province of Judeah.*

He was to be the last child of a family that already had numerous sons and daughters. Like his brothers, he would grow up to be a shepherd of his father's sheep, and perhaps later in life, the shepherd of his own flock. Actually, he would not quite grow up before working the sheep. By the time he was eight or nine he was doing simple chores, and finally the day came he had longed for. He was ten years old and could work in the fields with his brothers caring for the sheep.

It was a fine life and the little boy had a strong sense of accomplishment and well being as he worked day by day with his family. He was happy and a greatly loved boy who seemed to have a very caring heart to those who knew him. He had an unusual understanding of what was right and wrong, and although he was far from perfect in his behavior, his tendency and desire was to do the right thing as he interacted with his family, friends, and neighbors.

Although he came from a rather poor family, there was always enough to eat, with occasional extras when a few sheep were sold at the local market in Bethlehem.

But the best part of his young life was the yearly eight-mile journey to Jerusalem to celebrate Passover at the great holy temple. There he was in a different world of exciting shops and bazaars, seeing and meeting unusual people different from himself and his community, and seeing great buildings and palaces that always amazed him.

But the most wonderful place of all was the beautiful Jewish temple where his family brought their sacrifice to God. He would slip away from his family and wander throughout the magnificent temple exploring areas and rooms in which he was allowed access. He knew those mysterious places where he was not, the Holy Place and the Holy of Holies. But he would get as close to them as was permitted, and try to imagine what it looked like inside those holy walls.

Then, finally, he would search frantically for his family, knowing they would be upset with him for wandering off. He always found them and always received an earnest, yet loving, rebuke. What a wonderful time of year it was when he could go to the great city of Jerusalem and the beautiful temple of God.

But he also loved the fields and the sheep, and when he was there he felt a special closeness to the God he and his family worshiped, the great God of Abraham, Isaac, and Jacob.

On occasion he was allowed to stay with the flocks all night and that was a special time when he would sit near a small fire as his brothers would tell him exciting stories, most of which he knew were made up at the time of telling. Then gradually he would fall asleep, thinking about the exciting things he would do when he grew up.

One cool winter night something occurred that would define the rest of his life. He was just beginning to close his eyes in sleep when suddenly there was a bright light that lit up the ground around them, and before he and his brothers could scramble to their feet an angel appeared in front of them. In his entire life he had never known such fear. Yet with all the fear and trembling in his mind and body there was a wonderment, because he sensed the light was not a natural light, but a light from the Lord himself. God's glory was shining upon him. The angel spoke to them, saying:

"Do not be afraid,
I bring to you the most joyful news that has ever been told in all of history
And it is for all people everywhere.
For tonight in David's city, Bethlehem, there was born
The savior,
The Messiah,
The Lord.

And this shall be a sign for you to know where to find
the baby.
He will be wrapped in strips of cloth and lying in a
manger."

The little shepherd could hardly believe what was happening to him. He sat on the ground in stunned amazement. But there he was, in front of him, an angel, speaking,
it seemed, directly to him. And then all at once the sky was
filled with angels, thousands of them, all singing, singing a
sound of beautiful music he would never, ever forget. They
were singing to God and praising him. The words he heard
over and over were,

"Glory to God in the highest heaven
And on earth peace among men with whom he is well
pleased."

When they had finished singing, the angels left the shepherd boy and his brothers and returned to heaven. No one
moved.

In the still, crisp air of the Judean winter there was utter silence. What had they just witnessed? Why did the
angels come to tell us, lowly shepherds? Savior, Messiah,
Lord? What does all this mean? Thoughts that were pound-
ing in their minds and hearts.

And then the shepherd boy suddenly shouted out,
"Come on! Let's go to Bethlehem and see the baby!" As if
awakened from a dream his brothers shook themselves,
stood up and said to each other, "Yes, let's go and see this
wonderful thing that has happened tonight that the Lord
has told us about."

Running and stumbling they made their way to the small town of Bethlehem they knew so well, and after a short search found the baby and his mother and father in a cave that housed some cattle and donkeys and sheep. And there, just as the angel had said, was the baby lying in a manger wrapped in strips of cloth. Joseph and Mary, though startled at such a large group of visitors, asked them to come in and see their little baby boy. The shepherd boy managed to squeeze in front and knelt down by the manger and looked into the face of the little baby. Then he remembered what the angel had said,

That this little boy in front of him
Was
The savior of the world,
The Messiah,
His Lord.

And in the midst of being awe struck by that very idea, his next thought was "why did God pick me?" He could only wonder in silence.

Then Mary looked at him and asked, "Why did you come? How did you know about my son?"

And the little shepherd replied to Mary, "An angel told us to come."

His brothers also answered, "Yes, an angel sent from God." There was more silence and Mary and Joseph looked at each other. And the donkeys and cattle and a few sheep called out their quiet sounds.

Mary looked at the shepherd boy again and asked, "Would you like to know his name?"

"Yes, very much," he answered.

"His name is Jesus," Mary said.

"Oh," said the shepherd boy.

Mary then asked him, "Would you like to hold Jesus?"

"Yes!" he almost shouted, "Yes!"

Then he looked down at his hands and with a tear coming down his cheek said, "My hands are dirty. I cannot hold the Messiah with dirty hands."

And again Mary looked at Joseph in amazement.

Mary answered him, "It is all right. Do not worry about your hands."

Again he answered, "No, I cannot. My hands are dirty. I cannot hold my Lord with dirty hands."

Then Joseph got up and went to a pitcher of water and took a rag and wet it and went over to the little boy and washed his hands until they were clean. Then he looked down into his face and said, "Now you can hold my son and God's son."

And it did come to pass that the shepherd boy held the little baby in his arms and rocked him until the savior, the Messiah, the Lord fell asleep. When it was time for the shepherds to leave the child, for it was nearly midnight, the shepherd boy leaned down and kissed little Jesus on his cheek and said goodbye. Mary touched his arm and said, "Please come back when you can and see Jesus." The little boy smiled eagerly and said, "I will, maybe tomorrow."

Then the shepherds returned to their flocks with a wonderful story to tell and beginning the next morning they told everyone they met. Within a day or two the entire region had heard the amazing news that angels had come and told local shepherds that the Messiah had finally come as a baby born in a humble stable to poor parents.

Many believed the story but most scoffed because the Messiah they were expecting certainly would not be born in a smelly, dirty, dark stable. Their Messiah was coming as a king to boot out the cursed Romans. They knew well the Old Testament book of Isaiah and its prophecy.

> For unto us a child is born; unto us a son is given;
> And the government shall be upon his shoulder.
> These will be his royal titles:
> "Wonderful,"
> "Counselor,"
> "The Mighty God,"
> "The Everlasting Father,"
> "The Prince of Peace."
> His ever expanding government will never end.
> He will rule in perfect fairness and justice from the throne of his father David.
> He will bring true justice and peace to all the nations of the world.
> This is going to happen because the Lord of Heaven's armies
> Has dedicated himself to do it.

That's who their Messiah was to be, all right, a ruler of their government, not a subservient lackey to a despised Roman government. He would bring peace and justice to all nations and lead the Jewish people to prominence again among these nations. No, their ruler would never be born to a carpenter's wife in a lowly stable. Not what they wanted!

The next day the shepherd boy came again to the stable cave and found Joseph, Mary, and Jesus there, because there was still no room available in any of the inns and homes in the town. But that was okay, for as Joseph said, the rent was right.

Again the boy rocked the little baby and enjoyed his softness and his quiet cries and noises. He felt an overwhelming love for the baby Jesus and certainly there was always present in his mind the angels proclamation that this baby was the Messiah, the savior of the world, the one who would surely lead his country out of its domination by the awful Romans, whom he and his brothers hated.

The next time he returned to the stable, a few days later, he found it empty except for the animals. Inquiring of the innkeeper who owned the stable, he learned where Joseph, Mary, and Jesus were now living. After a short search he found them in a modest house on the outskirts of Bethlehem. Joseph had found work, Mary told him, and they would be living in Bethlehem for the indefinite future, rather than returning to Nazareth where they had lived before the birth of Jesus.

This was exciting news for the shepherd boy. He loved playing and talking to Jesus and rocking him to sleep in his arms. He also liked the special attention he received from Mary and Joseph. They were very fine people, he thought.

Over the next year the boy visited as often as he was able. His chores and tending the sheep took a good deal of his time so he could not go as often as he would have liked. But nearly once a week he would take the rocky path down from the hills to the town and out to the house where Jesus lived. It was fun to see Jesus grow and doing new things, smiling and cooing, crawling, standing, and finally his first step. Yes, it was great fun to be a small part of Jesus' life and family.

One of the little shepherd's favorite times was before he fell asleep out in the hills while tending the sheep. He would look up into the night sky and watch the stars and their different formations. In his imagination he created animals and people and all sorts of objects like the big and little dippers. As the seasons changed so did the stars in their locations in the night sky. Even at the age of twelve he knew well the major stars and their places in the heavens. They were like old friends to him.

Then one evening in late winter season, after chores were done, he laid back on his bed roll and began to study his stars. It was then that he noticed a large star he did not recognize. Strange, he thought, why he had not seen it before. As he stared at the new star, it appeared to grow until it was by far the largest star in the night sky. Where did it come from? He asked his brothers and they expressed their amazement as well.

For an hour or two they looked at the star and considered its meaning. Something this significant always had meaning. He knew that. But even this magnificent star could not keep his tired eyes from closing, and as he slept he dreamed of the star and the reason for its being. Two days later he knew the answer.

It was late afternoon and he had received permission from his father to go into Bethlehem, purchase a needed item at the market for the family, and, if he wanted, to visit Jesus for a short time. Of course he wanted to and he was soon running and skipping along the path to Bethlehem.

As he came to the main road that led into the town he saw a rather amazing sight. Coming up the road was a caravan of many men, some riding camels and donkeys, some walking, but creating a most unusual spectacle for the small town of Bethlehem. He could tell they were not just ordinary traders like he saw in Jerusalem. Some very important people were riding those camels. Look at how fine they were dressed and what elaborate riggings they had to ride on. Very impressive and exciting.

Maybe Jesus would have to wait a day or two. He really had to know where they were going. He knew he had no choice. Follow them he would. Follow them he did. Right to the house of Joseph, Mary, and Jesus he followed them. And to his disbelief that is where they stopped.

One of the servants dismounted and knocked on the door. In a moment Joseph appeared, and after a short discussion the beautifully dressed camel riders also dismounted and entered the house, followed closely and quickly by the little shepherd boy, acting as if he, too, belonged to the house. Shyness and timidity were not among his attributes.

This time, however, he stayed behind the richly dressed men as they entered the small room where Mary was holding the squirming and squealing Jesus in her arms. They stared at the noisy baby for a moment and then almost as if on signal dropped to their knees, bowing their heads to the floor in worship of the child.

For many seconds that seemed like forever to the shepherd boy, their heads remained bowed. There was utter silence in the room. Even Jesus stopped his noises and looked at the men in silence and curiosity. Slowly they raised upright on their knees. One motioned to servants in the room behind them who brought gifts and gave them to their kneeling masters. Then with extreme reverence they laid the gifts on the floor in front of Mary and Jesus, and Joseph, who stood nearby.

One of them spoke. "These gifts are for this child, whom we worship, for he is the Messiah, King of the Jews."

Then they opened the three gifts and once more bowed low. As they did the little boy could see the gifts and with eyes wide with amazement saw that one of the gifts was gold, much gold. He did not know what the other two were but they had to be valuable if they came with gold, he thought.

Another of the men spoke. "We saw his star where we live in eastern lands and it led us for many months to this place and this child. We praise God for this great honor of seeing and worshiping the Messiah today."

Once more they bowed their heads to the floor. Then they slowly and reverently backed out of the room while their eyes stayed on Jesus. The shepherd boy looked into their faces and saw tears flowing from their eyes, but their expressions were ones of utter joy and peace.

When they had left there was again a quiet stillness in the room. No one spoke. The little boy left the corner of the room where he had been standing and slowly walked to where Jesus was being held by Mary. There he fell on his knees, bowing his head to the floor and said, "I worship you, Jesus, my Lord."

In a few moments he stood, and like the richly clothed men before him, backed out of the room. Then he walked back to his home, with tears in his eyes and joy and peace in his heart. He too had seen the star of Bethlehem and had worshiped Jesus. He did, however, forget to buy the peppers for the family supper.

For the next two days the shepherd boy was full of happiness as he told his family and neighbors what he had seen and heard in Bethlehem that day and how he too had worshipped the Messiah. They listened with full attention as he told of these unusual rich men who had come to their town on such a strange mission, and of the gifts they had presented to Jesus with such regal reverence.

The following day the boy returned to the house of Joseph, Mary, and Jesus, but found they had left with all their belongings. Neighbors said they must have gone at night and quietly too, for no one saw or heard them leave. The shepherd boy was greatly saddened as he trudged back to his home to tell this news.

His days of joy and happiness had changed to sadness and then his time of sadness turned to a time of terror.

Into Bethlehem on a horrible day they marched. Two companies of Roman soldiers came marching, came marching to kill. Dividing into small groups, going house to house, killing, killing, killing. Children, two years and under. Mistakes, three, four and under. Mothers wailing, fathers sobbing, children in panic. Killing, killing until the right ones are dead. Killing so the right one is dead. "This King of the Jews, we got him! We are sure. Very thorough. Every house in Bethlehem and its countryside searched thoroughly. No sir, we missed no one. All dead!"

The shepherd boy saw some of it. Saw his little cousin, Benjamin, slaughtered and thrown on the ground, and a neighbor boy too. From a heart filled with happiness a few short days ago now swelled fury and hatred that seemed to grow as every hour passed. If he could he would kill every Roman on earth, he thought. Someday he would, he thought again.

As the days passed his fury lessened, for peaked fury can be sustained only so long. But his hatred was unchanging. It became part of his being. The only consolation he gave himself was time, the time for Jesus, the Messiah, the anointed one, the King of the Jews, to grow to manhood and reign as king and defeat and destroy the Roman scourge from his county for all time.

He knew that Jesus was not dead. He knew God had told his parents to leave in time. He knew it. He just knew it. God, make it true.

The years passed. The little shepherd boy grew into a man. He married, had ten children, five boys and five girls, by the time he was forty. Miraculously, all survived, and for that he was forever grateful to God and his wife. His dreams of killing Romans was still active in his mind, but responsibilities to his family and his own flocks kept them only dreams.

The hatred, however, remained. His prayer, nearly a daily prayer, was that his Messiah, he knew without doubt had come, would grow up and bring salvation to himself and his people from the hated Roman Empire.

One evening in the forty-third year of his life, the shepherd sat by a campfire with four of his five sons. His youngest, only six, would have to wait a few more years to join them. He still loved being in the fields with his flocks under the beautiful night sky, where brilliant stars shown down reminding him always of the time angels came down from

God. Of the time the great star shone so mysteriously and brought wealthy men from eastern lands to worship Jesus. Such wonderful memories.

But after those thoughts, without fail came those of Jesus and his family disappearing in the night, the child killings by Herod, the rage and hatred he felt against the Romans, which he knew he still had in his heart and always would. Such a paradox of thoughts when he gazed at the stars.

His mind turned to Jesus as it often did at night. He had to be thirty-three years old by now. What has he been doing all these years, especially his adult years? When was the Messiah, the King of the Jews, going to act like the King of the Jews? The shepherd admitted to himself that he was not an especially patient man. And he supposed he should not be second guessing God. Probably not!

From time to time someone would come along claiming to be the "messiah," and eventually something would turn up to show him to be a fraud. Or his followers would lose interest and he would disappear from his public stage. Or he would be killed. Whichever.

There was one now, he had heard, up around Galilee. It was said that he had turned water into wine at a wedding in Cana. Now that was a fancy trick! But also people had been healed and the crowds were warming to him. Rather a strange way for a Messiah to start in business, he thought. But as he knew, God did operate in mysterious ways.

He would have to keep his ears open on this one and find out the fellow's name and background. It was certainly time for Jesus to make his move. No doubt about that, he thought, as he begin to doze into a peaceful sleep under the dazzling stars he loved so much.

A few weeks later a small trading caravan stopped near his flocks to purchase a sheep or two to be slaughtered for their evening supper. After the bargaining and trading was complete, they spent a few minutes sharing gossip and news that might be of interest to either side of the bargaining table. Just before leaving, the caravan leader said, "I suppose you've heard about the miracle worker up around Galilee way?" "Only a little," replied the shepherd, with renewed interest. "What is his name and where is he from? What is he like."

The caravan leader answered, "His name is Jesus and he's from Nazareth. They say he came from Egypt as a small boy, but he was born in your town, here at Bethlehem. He's been healing people and casting out demons. Causing quite a stir with the people up there. Probably just another one of those prophets that make a big scene and then forgotten. No big deal. Well, must be going. Thanks again for the trade."

A person may pray and hope for months, years, and even decades for an event to occur, and when it suddenly happens the shock that it actually did may cause, for a time at least, an almost unbelief in its reality. For years the shepherd had been praying for Jesus to reveal himself, and suddenly the reality of this possibility was nearly more than he could bear. It was not that he had failed to believe Jesus would reappear, but rather that the time may have come and it was now.

That evening he talked to his wife, sons, and daughters about the news of the caravan leader. His children had heard the story of the angels, the men from the eastern lands, Jesus, Mary, and, Joseph, since they were old enough to listen, and his wife nearly from the time of their first meeting. It was decided he had to go to Galilee to meet this man to see if he were the Jesus of his youth, the Messiah, and the future King of the Jews. And so when the next caravan of traders came through Bethlehem headed for Galilee, the shepherd attached himself to them, at the cost of one sheep. Six long, hot days later he arrived at the town of Capernaum on the Sea of Galilee.

In the morning following his arrival he began to search the town and ask questions about the Jesus that healed. Everyone knew who he was talking about and told wonderful stories of healing and demons being driven out. But no one knew exactly the whereabouts of the healer.

Finally, in the early evening he saw a large crowd gathered around a house with a large courtyard. Approaching a man on the edge of the crowd, the shepherd asked what was happening inside. His reply was that a man by the name of Jesus was there and healing all who came to him. Now the shepherd was very excited and tried to push his way into the courtyard. After receiving numerous curses and dirty looks he finally made it to the edge of a small opening where several men were standing.

One was speaking to another while the others watched. Suddenly, the man being spoken to, shouted, "I can see! I can see!" The man next to the shepherd said, "Amazing, He lives down the road from me. He's been blind for twenty years. This Jesus has been healing like this for the past hour or two."

Finally, when there were no others there for healing, the crowd began to disburse and Jesus and the four men with him started to go into the house.

As they were about to enter the shepherd called out, "Jesus, my Lord."

Jesus turned around and asked, "Why do you call me Lord?"

"Because I believe you may be," replied the shepherd. "Please sir, where were you born and what is your age? And what are your parent's names?"

Jesus smiled and answered, "Strange questions but certainly answerable ones. I was born in Bethlehem of Judea. I am thirty-three years of age. My mother's name is Mary and my father, who is with God, was Joseph."

His knees buckled and whether he intended to fall on them at that moment or not, he did, and for the second time in his life bowed his head to the ground and repeated the words, "I worship you, Jesus, my Lord."

Jesus motioned for his followers to enter the house and he and the shepherd were alone in the now quiet courtyard. Jesus spoke, "Please sit here beside me. We have met before, many years ago."

"Yes," replied the shepherd. "You were a baby, born in a stable. Angels came to tell us. We went to see you. I rocked you to sleep on your first night on earth. For over a year I came to play with you. We had such fun times. Then you and your mother and father left, suddenly, and I never saw you again, until today."

"Am I what you expected?" asked Jesus.

"I did not know what to expect for certain, but I have prayed for your return as king," answered the shepherd.

"King of what?" asked Jesus.

"Why, king of all Israel, my Lord!" he exclaimed.

"Who am I?" Jesus asked quietly.

"You are the Messiah, the anointed one we have been waiting for. You are the savior of the world. The angel told us that, and then thousands of angels sang the most beautiful music I have ever heard."

"You answer well," Jesus said. "And why am I here?"

"You are to deliver Israel from the hated Romans, to restore our country to peace and justice, to rule our country as king, King of the Jews," the shepherd answered triumphantly.

Jesus quietly spoke. "My friend, the kingdom I am to rule is not of this world. It is the kingdom of your heart. What rules your heart and mind is what is important eternally. The Romans can hurt your body, but they cannot hurt your soul, unless you let them. My dear friend, do not hate the Romans. To hate is to hurt your own self."

The shepherd answered, "How can I not hate them! Look, my Lord, at all the horrible things they have done to the Jews. When you were a little one in Bethlehem they butchered all those children. They almost killed you as well, but God saved you."

"There are evil Romans as there are evil Jews," replied Jesus. We need to warn them of evil ways. We need to pray for them. We even need to love them. But we must never hate or kill them. God changes hearts and minds. We are to obey him. My dearest friend, the children killed are with God. What of Roman souls?"

The shepherd silently pondered Jesus' words. They were strange to him. Strange even coming from the lips of his Lord. So easy to say forgive, but beyond his understanding, beyond his willingness. Too much hate. Too long a time. Disappointed, let down, and discouraged, he started to leave. But Jesus called to him, "Come in and have supper with us before you leave. I have some friends I would like you to meet."

On the long walk home he thought of many things. Yes, Jesus' ideas would be fine if they worked. Love and peace were a lot easier to live with then hate and war. But he doubted they would work. He knew the Romans pretty well, he thought, and warning them of their evil ways would probably bring laughter at best and a sword in the stomach at worse. As for loving them, he wasn't sure they knew what love was, and would likely interpret it to be weakness, anyway. But he was certainly willing for Jesus to give it a try. He was, after all, the Messiah. He should know things other men did not. Besides, what choice did he, a shepherd, have.

And those four followers of his certainly were not military types, to say the least! Right off the boat, as it were! Especially that Peter fellow. Impetuous and really squirrelly. Anything he led would be disastrous. Maybe he would check back with Jesus in a year of so. Meanwhile, it would be good to be home.

It was good to be back with his family, whom he loved. They were so glad to see him. Nearly two weeks was a long time to be gone. Lucky for him he had strong, good sons to watch his flocks and a smart loving wife to manage the household. Yes, he was a fortunate man. Life was good. God was good.

They waited patiently until he finished a huge supper and then he told them about Jesus. What they had heard was true. He saw Jesus do many miracles and even talked to him alone and at supper. But what he had hoped to hear, he did not, and that was very disappointing. But he still had hope. Jesus was just starting out and he would see the need for realistic action eventually, he was quite sure. He hoped.

And so, after a night's rest, it was back to his sheep and the fields and the wonderful life he loved.

Over the next year more and more news came down from the north, telling of the miracles and healings of Jesus. But it also told of his problems with the Jewish religious leaders. His healings on the Sabbath and forgiving men's sins would not be welcomed by the higher ups, that the shepherd knew for sure. Of course, if they did not believe him to be the Messiah, which they did not, one could hardly fault them. He could hardly blame them for not believing. He probably would not either, if he were honest about it, if an angel and then thousands of angels had not told him in person. It was a little frustrating, he told himself. Jesus was making enemies of his own people rather than the Roman scum.

More and more the urge to return to Galilee was being felt by the shepherd. He knew many people from all around Jerusalem were flocking there to see Jesus. Perhaps it was time he returned. Yes, it really was. He would leave within the week, he thought!

It was not long before he found a group of travelers and many of them were going to see the teacher and healer, Jesus. The journey took less time than caravan travel and he was in Capernaum in four long, hot days. He also saved the cost of one sheep.

The following morning he started his search for Jesus. He noticed hundreds of people streaming up into the small hills outside the town. Following them for almost a mile he came to an immense crowd of thousands of men, women, and children, some sitting, some standing, many milling around, and all talking it seemed. Utter confusion.

After a short time the huge gathering gradually became less noisy. He turned and then he saw him. Jesus and a group of his followers were walking through the crowd up to the crest of a hill overlooking the awaiting throng. Now this is more like it, the shepherd thought. There had to be eight or ten thousand people here, if you counted everyone. Not an army, certainly, but if he could draw this many people to hear preaching, think of how many fighters he could get to go against the hated Romans. He had underestimated Jesus after all, he thought with a smile.

The morning was perfect. The air was cool and still. The sun was shining. The crowd became instantly silent. In a voice that was both subdued, yet strong enough for the crowd to hear easily, Jesus began to speak, seemingly to his disciples. He taught them:

"Humble men are blessed and fortunate,
for the Kingdom of Heaven is given to them."

"Those who mourn are also blessed,
because God will comfort them."

"Even the meek and lowly are blessed,
for the whole world belongs to them."

The shepherd was not too sure about that one.

"If one desires to be just and good,
he will be satisfied."

"If a person is kind and merciful,
they will be shown mercy."

Nor that one.

"Those with pure hearts shall see God."

"Peacemakers shall be called the sons of God."

"Those persecuted because they are good will be blessed
for the Kingdom of Heaven will be theirs."

"When one is reviled, persecuted and lied about, because he is a follower of Jesus,
be happy about it because a great award awaits you in
heaven."

That's fine, too, thought the shepherd, but what about
the here and now? How does all this apply to the Roman
problem?

As Jesus continued to teach, the crowds listened with
rapt attention, including the shepherd. He agreed with most
of Jesus' teachings until he started talking about how to
respond to violence and abuse. Jesus said not to resist violence. If you get slapped on the cheek, turn the other so it
can get slapped too. If you are ordered to give up your shirt,
then give up your coat as well. If a Roman soldier requires
you to carry his gear one mile, carry it two miles. The shep-

herd had been ordered to carry a Roman officer's gear two years ago. It was a law that had to be obeyed. But two miles? No thank you! One was humiliating enough.

Jesus continued.

> "Love your enemies," he said. "Pray for those who persecute you.
> In that way you will be acting as true sons of your Father in heaven.
> If you love only those who love you, what good is that?
> Even bad men manage that."

The shepherd knew he was talking about the Romans most of all. He remembered what Jesus had said during their meeting a year before, about not hating the Romans, to pray for them, and to even love them. It was hard to conceive of such a task, much less honestly do it.

His favorite teaching, however, came in the late morning when Jesus taught about prayer. He said,

> "Ask, and you will be given what you ask for.
> Seek, and you will find.
> Knock and the door will be opened.
> For everyone who asks, receives.
> Anyone who seeks, finds.
> If only you will knock, the door will open."

Now that was a good teaching, he thought. He could relate to that one. He had been praying for Jesus, the Messiah, to become King of the Jews for thirty-five years! And

God's answer was coming closer all the time. He hoped. It was one of the favorites of the crowd as well.

Near the end of his great teaching, Jesus talked about heaven. He said,

"Heaven can be entered only through a narrow gate.
The highway to hell is broad, and its gate is wide enough
For all the multitudes who choose its easy way.
But the gateway to life is small, and the road is narrow,
And only a few ever find it."

On the broad highway to hell there are many ways by which people have chosen to go to heaven. The narrow road with the narrow gate has God's way of going to heaven. Jesus continued,

"Not all who sound religious are really godly people.
They may refer to me as 'Lord,'
But will still not get to heaven."

The shepherd was surprised at this teaching. He thought all religious people who believe in God would go to heaven. He observed the Sabbath, went to the synagogue, and was good to his family and neighbors. He certainly knew God's son. He had talked with him and even had supper with him. He was present with him almost at the hour of his birth. Oh, he knew that he sinned in many ways, but they were not that serious, were they?

And when Jesus was finished and began to leave the place he was teaching, the shepherd followed him as closely as he could. Suddenly, a man with leprosy approached Jesus. The crowd pulled back in fear.

He knelt before Jesus and pleaded, "If you want to, you can heal me."

Jesus touched the man and said, "I want to. Be healed."

And instantly the leprosy disappeared. And the crowd and the shepherd were amazed at the power and love of Jesus.

Coming into Capernaum a Roman army officer, who was a centurion in rank, approached Jesus. Oh, here comes trouble, thought the shepherd. But to the great surprise of the shepherd and the crowd, the Roman centurion began to plead with Jesus to come to his home and heal his servant boy who was paralyzed and filled with pain. Jesus answered, "Yes, I will come and heal him."

Then the centurion said,

"Sir, I am not worthy to have you in my home,
And it is not necessary for you to come.
If you will only stand here and say, 'Be healed,' my servant will get well.
I know, because I am under the authority of my superior officers
And I have authority over my soldiers, and I say to one, 'Go,' and he goes,
And to another, 'Come,' and he comes,
And to my slave boy, 'Do this or do that,' and he does it.
And I know you have the authority to tell his sickness to go and it will go!"

Jesus stood there amazed. Turning to the crowd he said,

"I have not seen such faith like this in all the land of Israel!

And I tell you this, that many Gentiles like this Roman
officer,
Shall come from all over the world and sit down in the
kingdom of heaven,
With Abraham, Isaac, and Jacob.
And many an Israelite, those for whom the kingdom was
prepared,
Shall be cast into outer darkness,
Into a place of weeping and torment."

Then Jesus said to the Roman officer, "Go on home.
What you have believed has happened!"

The shepherd later heard that the servant boy was healed
at that same hour.

The shepherd was confused. He knew he was and that
bothered him. Jesus was not what he was supposed to be.
Events were not happening that should be happening. A
hardened Roman centurion should not come begging to a
Jew for help. And for what? To save a servant boy!

And what did Jesus mean when he said a bunch of for-
eign Gentiles from all over the world would be allowed in
the kingdom of heaven with Abraham, Isaac, and Jacob, no
less! And some Jews would not be in heaven? Well, he knew
a few that shouldn't be, he supposed. But that's what the
kingdom of heaven was for, the Jews, Wasn't it? Wasn't it?

And where did he fit into this new picture that was
emerging? How did all this pertain to him? Some religious
people will not get into heaven? Scary!

He soon caught up with Jesus and his followers and
he was warmly welcomed, and invited to eat the evening
meal with them. This greatly pleased him. Not only did

he want to talk with Jesus, but he wanted to find out the thinking of the rest of his followers on things he had seen and heard that day.

As the meal was prepared they gathered, talking in small groups. A tall, rather tough-looking man came up to the shepherd and welcomed him in a friendly way and introduced himself as Judas. He asked how he had come to know Jesus, and when told the story by the shepherd, he seemed surprised yet fascinated by it. He questioned the shepherd about the details of the angels coming down from heaven, The visit of the rich men from the east, and the murder of the children by King Herod.

The shepherd told of his years of praying that Jesus would reveal himself as King of the Jews and lead the revolt against the Romans. When he mentioned this, Judas put his hand on his shoulder and with eyes widened said, "We share the same dream my friend, as do several others with us. Continue praying that Jesus will soon see the need as well."

Later in the evening the shepherd did talk to Jesus and some of his other followers. Jesus talked about the Roman officer and how his faith to believe was the crucial issue. He told the shepherd that the kingdom of heaven was open to all people who had this kind of faith in him. But when the shepherd talked with his followers, he sensed that they and Jesus were not thinking the same on some of these issues. They did not seem to understand what Jesus was teaching them. Neither did he, for that matter, he admitted to himself.

The next day he began the long walk home and thought about all he had seen and heard. He was still disturbed by the direction Jesus was headed, but he was beginning to understand a little of that direction, even though it was not to his liking. Not at all to his liking, he thought.

Over the next year and a half, news continued to reach the shepherd, telling of the happenings in the life of the famous healer and teacher.

As he worked in the fields or lay under his stars at night, the shepherd had much time to ponder the words Jesus had spoken and what they might mean to him and his nation. He was beginning to suspect, in the deep recesses of his mind, that perhaps Jesus' thoughts about life and living on this earth were different than his.

With this came questions of his relationship to God and what part sin in his life mattered to that relationship. He had always admitted to himself that he was far from perfect, but certainly as good a person as most of the people he knew in his life. But, nevertheless, he would still like to know what God thought of his trivial sins. Maybe he would ask Jesus the next time he saw him.

The time came sooner then he expected, for during the following week news came to Bethlehem that Jesus was in Jericho and heading toward Jerusalem. And so very early on the following Sunday morning the shepherd left on the short three-hour walk to Jerusalem. He was not alone, for many of the Jewish faithful were coming to Jerusalem in preparation for the holy day of Passover later in the week.

Arriving midmorning, the shepherd recalled memories of the great city from his youth and his family's annual pilgrimage to the great temple of God. It was good to be here again, he thought. Such wonderful times!

Within the hour of arriving he began to hear loud shouts coming from the city gate where he had just entered. "He's coming! He's coming! Jesus is coming!"

Running through the gate with the crowd, he saw in the distance an immense mob yelling and shouting around a man riding a small donkey. As they came closer, he saw it was Jesus on the small animal. And amazingly, people were cutting branches from palm trees and laying them in front of his path as he proceeded toward the gate of the city.

Someone near him yelled, "Did you hear? Jesus has declared himself King of the Jews! There is going to be a revolution! Hallelujah!"

And those nearby took up the cry, "Hosanna to the Son of David!"

"Blessed is he who comes in the name of the Lord!"

"Hosanna in the highest."

"God's man is here!"

The shepherd could not believe his eyes and ears. What he had prayed for years was coming to pass! Now! Today! And he had such doubts. But no more! This was real. He knew it!

Jesus was coming into Jerusalem and the crowds were getting larger and larger. They were heading toward the temple. The revolution would begin there! Of course! And the shepherd took up the cry of "Hosanna, Hosanna to Jesus."

He spotted Judas in the crowd and worked his way over to him. "My friend, Judas Iscariot, wonderful day is it not?" yelled the shepherd over the shouting crowd.

Judas answered, "My friend, good to see you! Yes, it is a promising day. A day to give thanks for."

"Can he pull it off?" asked the shepherd. "Will the people make him king? Can I help?"

"It will depend on how goes the mood of the people. They are so fickle. They want a revolution, but they are afraid. I believe they will need a push more than Jesus is capable or willing to do. But stay close. Perhaps you can play a part."

By then they had reached the temple and entered the Court of the Gentiles, where the non-Jews worship God. There money changers and sellers of animals for sacrifice were set up to do business. Actually, it was the business of cheating visitors who came to offer sacrifice and worship God. A dirty business, nearly everyone agreed, but business was business and the temple was the biggest business in town.

Then to his disciples surprise and certainly the shepherd, Jesus began driving out the money changers and sellers of animals from their booths and turning over tables and letting animals loose, and causing immense chaos in the temple court.

Jesus kept crying out for all to hear,

"The Scriptures declare, my temple is a place of prayer,
But you have turned it into a den of thieves."

But even so, amid all the chaos, the blind, crippled, and sick came to Jesus and he healed them all.

The scene the shepherd observed was that of two extremes of emotion. Rejoicing and love by those healed, anger and hatred by the money changers and animal sellers. Bedlam reigned.

Then the shepherd noticed standing against one of the temple walls many of the chief priests and Jewish leaders, and in their eyes he had never seen such hatred. A cold chill ran though his body. He felt he was as close to evil as he could possibly be.

Judas came over to him. "You see them, too," he said. "They mean trouble, real trouble." He paused and then said, "The story you told me about the angels and the rich men from the east. You did not just make that up or imagine it, did you? It was over thirty-five years ago, after all."

"Of course not," replied the shepherd. "It is more real than you standing beside me right now. It is as vivid to me today as then."

"Good," said Judas. "That has to pretty well prove he is the Messiah, the son of God. The priests cannot kill him since that is the case. Listen carefully," he said quietly. "This is what we are going to do. We need to help the Jewish authorities arrest him. That will accomplish two objectives. It will force Jesus to take control of the situation and it may incite the people to rebel. As things are going now, nothing is going to happen. He's doing the same as he has always done, healing people and making the Jewish leaders angry. We must do something!"

"We cannot have the Lord arrested," exclaimed the shepherd. "That would be evil and wrong. I cannot do that and neither should you. You must not!"

Judas looked at the shepherd and after a short pause said, "Yes, I suppose you are right." Then he walked away.

For the next few days the shepherd stayed with Jesus and his followers. What he heard and observed began to change his life and the way he viewed his world, God, and himself.

He remembered the Pharisee lawyer who asked Jesus, "which is the most important command in the law of Moses?"

Jesus had replied,

"Love the Lord your God with all your heart, soul, and, mind.
This is the first and greatest commandment.
The second most important is similar: Love your neighbor as much as you love yourself.
All the other commandments and all the demands of the prophets
Stem from these two laws and are fulfilled if you obey them.
Keep only these and you will find you are obeying the others."

The shepherd thought to himself. Do I really love God like I should, or do I just use him at my convenience? Perhaps I want the wrong things from God. Do I only want Jesus so he can rid us of the Romans? Why did I come to see him? Why did he come to earth?

They were walking down a quiet road. Jesus was alone and the shepherd caught up and walked beside him in silence.

Jesus spoke, "We have come a long way since Bethlehem. Where are you on your journey?"

"I am not sure, my Lord. I thought I knew, but I think I do not. I am confused about why you are here on earth. I fear for my own sins and what they mean to you and God. I had prayed for you to come and save us from the Romans, but you have not, nor does it seem that you will."

"My son, I have come to save you from something much worse than Romans. I have come to save you from your sin."

"Lord, I have many sins for which I have great sorrow."

"My beloved son, your sorrow is wise and seen by God. For the sin that needs to be forgiven and removed lives now in your soul. This sin is the sinful nature of your soul. It condemns and keeps you from eternal life with your Heavenly Father."

The shepherd began to weep. "Oh Lord, I want my sins removed from my soul. I want to live forever with you and my Heavenly Father. How can my sins be forgiven?"

Jesus answered the shepherd, "In a few days I am going to be crucified on a Roman cross. I am going to pay the price of your sin by dying in your place."

"Oh, Lord, there must be another way."

"There is no other way but the shedding of my blood. For God so loved the world that he gave his only son so that anyone who believes in him shall not perish but have eternal life. I have come to seek and to save the lost. I have come to seek and to save you. You are why I am here. You are why I am going to die."

"Lord, I am lost and I need to be saved. Save me now."

"My dearest friend, I have."

Peace came to the shepherd at last.

The following day Jesus, his followers, and the shepherd were leaving the temple grounds. The sun was shining brightly and the great temple and the other temple buildings were magnificent as the sun shone on their beautifully designed and colorful stonework. Viewing Solomon's Porch, the shepherd was still amazed at its splendor and its length of over a quarter of a mile. The walk around the temple grounds was nearly one mile. Reconstruction of the temple complex had started several years before the shepherd was born and would continue until finished in 64 A.D. Thousands of workers for a good part of a century worked on this holy place of God. The shepherd still marveled at its beauty. Now it had an even deeper meaning as the place of worship for the God and savior he truly knew.

As the followers of Jesus were pointing out one spectacular sight after another, it seemed to the shepherd that Jesus had become saddened and quiet. Finally, the others began to notice as well and they slowly became silent.

Then he spoke, "Do you see all these beautiful buildings? I tell you the truth. All of them will be torn down. Not one stone will be left upon another."

The shepherd was stunned. How could this beautiful place be torn down? Why? Who could do such a thing? When? If this place is not permanent, what on earth is? What on earth is? And then the Holy Spirit spoke to his heart and mind to remind him that nothing is permanent on this earth. He remembered the words from the Book of Isaiah,

That man is like the grass that dies away,
And his beauty fades like the dying flowers.
The grass withers, the flower fades beneath the breath of God.
And so it is with fragile man.

The grass withers, the flowers fade,
But the Word of our God shall stand forever.

So few permanent and everlasting things. His Heavenly Father, Jesus, the Holy Scriptures, his soul, his soul.

On the first evening of Passover week Jesus and his twelve followers celebrated the Passover meal together, while the shepherd ate in the home of a relative in Jerusalem.

The Passover commemorates the night the Israelites were freed from Egypt after being in that land for 430 years. For many of those years they were slaves to pharaoh and the Egyptians. Finally, the time came for God to take the Israelites out of Egyptian bondage. When pharaoh refused to allow them to leave, God brought many plagues through Moses on the country of Egypt. But pharaoh still refused to let the Israelites go. Finally, Moses told pharaoh that all first born sons in Egypt would die if he did not let them go. He still stubbornly refused.

To protect the Israelites' firstborns, God said he would pass over all their homes marked by the blood of a lamb on their doorposts. That night all firstborn children of the Egyptians died and the children of the Israelites were saved. Saved by the blood of a lamb.

After the Passover meal the shepherd returned to be with Jesus and his followers. They walked to a garden grove called Gethsemane. While the others waited, Jesus took Peter, James, and John a short distance away to pray. The shepherd noticed that Judas was missing. That was strange, he thought, that Judas was not with Jesus on Passover night. For more than an hour Jesus prayed.

Suddenly, the shepherd heard noise and saw lighted torches of a large crowd coming into the garden. As they came closer he could tell the man leading them was Judas. Why was he there? What was he doing? The shepherd started toward Judas to greet him but the crowd headed directly toward Jesus. The shepherd continued toward Judas until both arrived at the same time where Jesus was standing.

"Judas," the shepherd yelled, "What is going on here?"

Judas did not answer but in a loud friendly voice said to Jesus, "Hello, Master." And then he embraced him.

The shepherd heard Jesus say to Judas, "Judas, how could you do this, betray the Messiah with a kiss? Go ahead and do what you have come for."

Then those with Judas seized Jesus. At that moment the shepherd, to his horror, realized what Judas had done. Suddenly, a sword slashed through the air. A cry of pain. A spurting of blood from the head of a man in the crowd. Jesus looked at Peter, holding a bloody sword in his hand, and spoke, "Put away your sword! Those using swords will get killed! Don't you realize that I could ask my Father for thousands of angels to protect us and he would send them instantly?" Then he touched the man's ear that had been severed and it was healed.

Jesus was led away by the crowd. The shepherd looked around for Peter or John or Matthew, or any of the others, but could find none of them. Had they all fled in fear? Fear he could understand for he was badly frightened and totally uncertain of what to do or where to go.

He prayed almost out loud, "Lord, tell me now what you want me to do." The past flooded into his mind. Angels, a baby in a manger, the star, men from eastern lands, healings, the words of Jesus.

In an instant the Spirit of God gave him understanding. He would stay as close to his Lord as he could. He must show him that he was with him, that he loved him, and would never betray him. Jesus was going to die soon, for him, for his sins, on a terrible painful cross. Jesus needed him. He knew that. And if it were the last thing on earth he would ever do, he would not fail his Lord. He would not! He would not!

In the distance he saw the lighted torches leading Jesus toward the city gate that would take him into Jerusalem and perhaps away from him forever. Tripping and stumbling down through the darkened Kidron Valley, he ran, desperately trying to catch up before they disappeared into the sleeping city. Just as the gate was closing he darted in unchallenged.

The mob took Jesus to the home of Caiaphas, the high priest. The shepherd entered the large courtyard, where a large group of important-looking men were gathered. When he asked one of he mob who they were, he was gleefully informed that they were the entire Jewish Supreme Court, and they were going to get this Messiah for sure this time!

The court attempted to build a case against Jesus that would result in a death sentence, but the witnesses were so obviously lying that no credible case could be made. Finally two men were able to claim they heard Jesus say that he was able to destroy the temple of God and rebuild it in three days.

The high priest stood up and said to Jesus, "Well, what about it? Did you say it or didn't you?" But Jesus did not answer him. Then the high priest said to Jesus, "I demand in the name of the living God that you tell us whether you claim to be the Messiah, the Son of God."

"Yes," Jesus said, "I am. And in the future you will see me, the Messiah, sitting at the right hand of God and returning on the clouds of heaven."

At that the high priest tore his own clothing and shouted, "Blasphemy! What need have we for other witnesses? You have heard him say it! What is your verdict?"

The court shouted, "Death! Death! Death!"

Then those in the mob spat on his face, and struck him, and mocked him by saying, "Prophesy to us, you Messiah! Who struck you that time?"

The shepherd was devastated. Yes, in the way they were brutalizing Jesus, to be certain, but also these men were the leaders of his faith, of his religion, men he had always looked up to as good, religious, and godly. And now they were acting horribly, with evil hearts. Just look at the high priest leading this farce, this abominable example of religion gone bad. Then the thought struck him that they too needed Jesus to save them as much as he had. That they were as lost from God as the most heathen Gentile. The shepherd wept in the agony of what he was witnessing.

After a while he looked across the courtyard and saw Peter in a corner by himself. Walking over to him, he saw he was sobbing as if in a daze. He put his hand on his shoulder and Peter began to shake violently as if he were in terrible pain.

The shepherd said quietly, "I know you are suffering a terrible loss. So am I. Peter, he is going to die for us on a Roman cross. He told me." And when he said that the look he saw on Peter's face was that of a mad man.

He screamed out, "I denied him! I denied him! I denied him!" And he bolted from the shepherd and ran out of the courtyard into the coming dawn.

The shepherd chased after him yelling, "Peter, he will forgive you! He will forgive you!" Finally, in the darkened streets of Jerusalem the shepherd lost him and he began to walk slowly back to the courtyard. In the distance a rooster crowed.

That morning the council of Jewish leaders took Jesus in chains to Pilate, the Roman governor of Judea and Samaria. There before Pilate they accused him. "This fellow has been leading our people to ruin by telling them not to pay taxes to the Roman government, and by claiming he is our Messiah, a king."

Pilate asked Jesus, "Are you their Messiah, their king?"

"Yes," Jesus replied, "it is as you say."

Pilate then turned to Jesus' accusers and said, "So, that isn't a crime."

Terribly upset by this response, they replied, "But he is causing riots against the government everywhere he goes, all over Judea, from Galilee to Jerusalem."

"Is he then a Galilean?" Pilate asked. Finding that he was, Pilate instructed them to take Jesus to Herod whose jurisdiction was Galilee. Herod happened to be in Jerusalem at this time for Passover.

He was very happy to have the chance to see Jesus. He had heard much about him and he would love to see Jesus perform a miracle just for him. So Herod asked Jesus question after question, while the chief priests and other leaders were shouting their accusations. Jesus stood there saying nothing.

Finally, Herod and his soldiers began mocking and ridiculing Jesus, and before they sent him back to Pilate, put a kingly robe on him.

The shepherd was able to follow surprisingly close and witness both encounters with Pilate and Herod. Once he had caught Jesus' eye and he detected a slight smile come to his face. He was thankful Jesus saw him and would know he was not alone in his ordeal.

Jesus was once again brought before Pilate. And when he announced the verdict to the chief priests and other Jewish leaders and people present, including the shepherd, there was a massive roar of protest and anger. For this is what Pilate had said to them.

"You brought this man to me, accusing him of leading a revolt against the Roman Government. I have examined him thoroughly on this point and find him innocent. Herod came to the same conclusion and sent him back to us. Nothing this man has done calls for the death penalty. I will therefore have him scourged with leaded thongs, and release him."

But the maddened crowd continued to yell and scream, "Kill him and release Barabbas to us!"

Now Barabbas was in prison for starting a resurrection against Rome and for murder. It was Pilate's custom to release one of his Jewish prisoners at Passover time. Pilate argued that Jesus was the right prisoner to be released, not Barabbas. But the crowd would have none of that. "Crucify him! Crucify him!" they shouted.

Once again Pilate argued, "Why? What crime has he committed? I have found no reason to sentence him to death. I will therefore scourge him and let him go."

With that, the crowd began to get out of hand with their yelling and cursing and near-riot attitude. Over and over again they kept calling for Jesus to be crucified, until Pilate, whose position as governor was shaky with Rome anyway, relented and sentenced Jesus to die. He also released the murderer, Barabbas, to the people.

Pilate then had Jesus terribly scourged and beaten. Soldiers mocked him by stripping him and placing a scarlet robe on his torn back and a crown of thorns on his head. They placed a stick in his right hand as a scepter and knelt before him, saying "Hail, King of the Jews!" Then they spat on him and hit him with the stick he had held.

The shepherd had found a way into the armory and saw Jesus suffer this torture and degradation. He almost had to turn away but in the end he forced himself to watch the suffering, with tears streaming down his face.

Then they took him to be crucified the Roman way, on a heavy, wooden cross.

Who crucified Jesus? Who was to be responsible for his death? Romans? Jews? Gentiles? You? Me? All of us. Every human who will ever live crucified Jesus. The sins of us all were the reason he died. Even beyond that it was God who sent his son to die. It was God's plan, born out of his holy love for all mankind. Ultimately, God chose that Jesus should die. It was God's choice to sacrifice his son so the sins of men could be forgiven.

Through the narrow streets of Jerusalem they took him. The soldiers, the mob, his friends, the shepherd, you, me.

Stumbling, falling, suffering, carrying the cross himself, until he could carry it no longer. The shepherd saw him fall. He rushed to help but was quickly shoved aside by a soldier. Jesus struggled to pick up the cross again but his torture had weakened him and he could not. A man was grabbed from the crowd. Simon was his name from Cyrene in Africa. He was told to pick up that cross and follow that man, so that he could die on it at a place called Golgotha, outside the city walls on the execution grounds, the hill of torment, bleeding, suffering, dying.

A soldier offered Jesus a drugged wine. He tasted it and shook his head. "Suffer then," the soldier snarled.

They dropped the cross on the ground and threw Jesus on it, grabbed an arm, drove a spike through his hand and into the cross. Then the other hand. A leg was shoved on the cross, a spike hammered though the heel bone and into the wood. Then the other leg.

The shepherd tried to watch the hammering but in this he failed. With his body shaking he bowed his head and closed his eyes, and with clenched fists, wept in horror at the clanging of the nailing.

"All right, get it up," yelled the officer. Struggling, the soldiers dragged the cross to a hole, raised it up, and dropped it with a heavy thud into the ground. The shepherd heard it fall, and the cry of pain; he saw flesh tear, and blood flow.

Jesus had been crucified.

It was midmorning. The shepherd came closer to the cross. Close enough to hear Jesus pray, "Father, forgive these people. They do not know what they are doing."

To the left of him the shepherd saw the soldiers throwing dice to see who would get Jesus' cloak. He was amazed, because he realized the feelings he had for those soldiers were not that of hate and bitterness, but of love. He looked into the face of Jesus and saw a slight smile and nod. Then he fell on his knees and bowed his head to the ground and prayed, "Thank you, my Lord Jesus, thank you."

Pilate had a sign prepared and now a soldier nailed it to the cross above the head of Jesus. The Jewish leaders had not liked it but Pilate was not about to let them get their way twice, so he would not change it or take it down. He would show them! The sign read, "This is Jesus, King of the Jews"

Throughout the morning the Jewish leaders mocked Jesus and said such things as, "He was so good at helping others, let's see him save himself if he is really God's chosen one, the Messiah."

The soldiers yelled to him, "If you are the King of the Jews, save yourself." The shepherd wished he could tell them the story of the angels, the rich men from the east, how he had known most of his life that Jesus was God's son, the Messiah, the King of the Jews. Maybe they would believe. Maybe not. Maybe some would. Yes, some would.

The Romans had crucified two criminals on either side of Jesus. They were dying terrible, agonizing, angry deaths. But for a while, even in their pain, they scoffed at Jesus. "So you are the Messiah, are you? Prove it by saving yourself and us, too, while you're at it."

The shepherd noticed that after a while one of the criminals became quiet, while the other kept on ragging Jesus. Finally, the quiet one spoke. "Don't you even fear God when you are dying? We deserve to die for our evil deeds, but this man hasn't done one thing wrong. Then he looked at Jesus and said, "Jesus, remember me when you come into your kingdom."

And Jesus replied, "Today you will be with me in paradise. This is a solemn promise."

The shepherd heard it all and was astounded at the simplicity of this miracle that had occurred before him. A robber, who only an hour before was ridiculing Jesus, had admitted his sin, and had asked Jesus to allow him into heaven with him. And Jesus had promised that robber he would be with him in paradise.

"Why," thought the shepherd. "What qualifies that man hanging there for eternal life in heaven? What did he ever do to deserve it?" Then he realized that, of course, he had done nothing to deserve heaven, any more than he himself did. That man had come to Jesus with the simplest faith possible, but it had been enough. All that was needed. He had truly repented of his sins to Jesus and asked Jesus to save him. That was all. Enough. Enough.

Noon time.

Darkness suddenly covered the land. Sunlight blotted out from the earth. Great fear penetrated the soldiers and onlookers. Uncertainty, confusion, terrible feelings. The shepherd felt extreme evil around him. Murmurs of fear mingled with words of hate. On and on it went for three hours: immense tension, horrible sorrow, great hate, prevailing evil in the air.

The shepherd stood before the cross in the nearly darkened afternoon. Death sounds were coming from the three men on the crosses. Small cries of pain, gasps; quiet, penetrating gasps for air, for breath, for life.

In his mind he knew Jesus was dying. Now into his heart and soul came the final realization that he was dying for him. The suffering was for him. The mutilation for him. The dripping blood for him. The broken body for him.

Onto his knees he fell as his eyes sought the face of Jesus in the darkness of the cross. "Thank you, Jesus, my Lord. I love you," the shepherd boy said to his Messiah.

It was mid-afternoon.

Jesus suddenly shouted, "My God, my God, why have you forsaken me?"

It was that moment Jesus took upon himself the sins of the world. And because God cannot be with sin, Jesus was separated from God, and his suffering was almost more than he could stand. Then Jesus—God who came in human form—died for you, me, and everyone who ever lived.

The earth shook with a great earthquake. Rocks were broken. The shepherd later heard that tombs were opened and many godly men and women who had died came back to life and were seen in Jerusalem before many people. The curtain separating the Holy of Holies from the Holy Place in the great temple split from top to bottom.

The soldiers and others present were terribly frightened by the earthquake, and from everything else that was happening. The captain exclaimed, "This surely was the son of God."

Then the sun slowly began to shine again as the afternoon edged toward evening. And because Sabbath began at sunset, the Jewish leaders requested the legs of the men crucified be broken so death would be hastened and they would not have to be hanging there on the Sabbath. So the soldiers broke the legs of the two robbers, but when they came to Jesus, they saw he was already dead. However, to make sure, one of the soldiers pierced his side with his spear and blood and water flowed out onto the ground.

The shepherd was in great sorrow, but relieved and thankful Jesus was not suffering anymore. Now he was becoming concerned about the body of his Lord. Who had the authority to take him down from the cross and give him a decent burial? He waited near the cross until evening came. Finally, several men, one of whom he recognized as a member of the Jewish Supreme Court that had condemned Jesus, came up to the cross.

The shepherd approached the richly dressed man, and said, "Sir, what will you do with my Lord?"

The man turned to the shepherd and asked, "Are you one of his disciples?"

"No," replied the shepherd, "but he is my Lord and savior. He is the Messiah."

"You speak the truth, my friend. I too am a follower and believer in Jesus. Yes, he is the Messiah, the son of God."

"But sir, you were on the court that condemned him."

"Yes, I was. I objected, but most were against me. They were wrong. May God have mercy on them. I have permission to take his body. I will place it in my personal tomb not far from here. Will you help us?"

"I want to, sir," replied the shepherd.

And so the men carefully lifted the cross out of the hole and gently lowered it to the ground. Removing Jesus from the cross was very difficult, and as they were pulling his bloody hands and feet from the heavy spikes the shepherd's eyes again filled with tears as he thought of the suffering Jesus had gone through for him.

He remembered as a boy, and later as a man, reading from the Book of Isaiah, written nearly one thousand years before. Suddenly many of its words came flooding back into his memory.

> We despised and rejected him,
> A man of sorrows acquainted with bitterest grief.
> Yet it was our grief he bore, our sorrows that weighed him down.
> He was wounded and bruised for our sins.
> He was beaten that we might have peace.
> He was lashed and we were healed.
>
> Everyone of us have strayed away like sheep.
> We left God's path to follow our own,
> Yet God laid on him the guilt and sins of everyone of us.
>
> He was oppressed and he was afflicted,
> Yet he never said a word.
> From prison and trial they led him away to his death.
> But who among the people realized it was their sin he was dying for,
> That he was suffering their punishment.
> He was buried like a criminal, but in a rich man's grave.

They wrapped his body in a linen cloth. Then the shepherd knelt and picked up the body of his Lord and once again held him in his arms. The distance from the place of crucifixion to the tomb was not far. The shepherd felt as if he were walking through a dream as he carried Jesus' body down the hill to the tomb of the rich man, the high Jewish official, Joseph of Arimathea.

Could this really be happening? Why did God place him at both the birthplace and death place of his Lord? What did God want from him, a common shepherd?

On he walked down from Golgotha, down from the killing ground to the place of rest, the place of tombs. They placed the body of Jesus in a tomb room carved into the side of a limestone cliff.

Another member of the Jewish leadership, named Nicodemus, brought spices for anointing the body. The shepherd watched as they saturated the linen cloth with the spices and then carefully wrapped Jesus' body according to the Jewish custom of burial. When they were finished, they left the tomb and together rolled the large stone that had been cut for that purpose, in front of its doorway.

After the others had gone the shepherd sat on a rock a short distance away and thought about all that had happened that horrible day. He knew Jesus had to die, and he knew why, now.

But sadness still filled his thoughts. For a long time he sat in silence until in the distance he heard men approaching. He recognized them as soldiers, not Roman, but temple police. They ignored him and went to the tomb where Jesus was and sealed the stone that had been placed in front of the doorway. And then they stayed.

The shepherd approached the soldier in charge. "Sir, may I ask why you are here at the tomb of Jesus?"

The soldier replied, "We want to make sure this 'messiah' does not come back to life like he said he would. In other words, we don't want anyone stealing the body. By the way, what are you doing here? You a friend of this Jesus?"

"Yes," answered the shepherd. "He is my friend. He is our Messiah. He is your Messiah, too. He died to save you and me from our sin."

The soldier was taken back by the abruptness of these words. "How do you know that? You can't know that!"

Then the shepherd told him the story of the angels, the baby in the manger, the star, and the wealthy men from the eastern lands. He told of his own experience of being lost and being found by Jesus. When he was finished the soldier looked at the ground.

"You really believe what you are saying." He paused. "I will think on your words." Again he paused. "Meanwhile, I will guard this tomb very carefully."

The shepherd started to leave and after a few steps heard the soldier's quiet voice. "Thank you for telling me." The shepherd turned and looked at the soldier and nodded.

As he walked away, the shepherd felt strongly that he needed to return home. He wanted to tell his family all that had happened to Jesus, and also what had happened to himself. He wanted them to know that Jesus had come to seek and to save them, too, and had died on the cross for their sins.

So he left Jerusalem, even though the Sabbath was beginning, and under a nearly full moon began the walk back to Bethlehem, where it had all begun so long ago.

It was late evening when he arrived and all his family who were not in the fields greeted him with many excited questions. As he told them the terrible, yet wonderful story, of all that had come to pass, they listened quietly. When he finished, he offered a prayer of thanksgiving to God for all that he had seen and heard, that he could share with his family all these things, and that Jesus was truly their savior, Lord, and Messiah. Then very weary, emotionally and physically, he slept. That night he dreamed of angels singing in heaven.

A few days later a small caravan of traders, coming from the north, stopped where the shepherd was tending his sheep, and as often done in the past, bargained for a couple of sheep. The shepherd, after the trading was finished, asked if they had heard about Jesus, who was crucified.

"Sure have," answered the trader. "The rumor is that the body of Jesus is missing from the tomb it was placed in. His followers say he has risen from the dead and is alive. The temple leaders claim the guards all fell asleep and his followers stole the body. But that sounds kind of fishy to me. There was a huge gravestone that had to be rolled away And that in itself makes noise. Someone is lying."

"Yes," thought the shepherd, "And I know who it is!"

Within the week he was in Jerusalem searching for Jesus, his followers, anyone who would help him find his Lord. For three days he searched without success. Finally, while eating on a bench in a marketplace, where he had purchased his lunch, the shepherd spotted a familiar face. It was Peter, walking in his direction. He called out, "Simon Peter!" Upon hearing his name, Peter stopped, appeared startled, and uncertain how to react. Then he saw the shepherd and came over to him, smiling.

"My good friend, it is good to see you again. I have wonderful news. Jesus is alive! He returned from the dead just as he said he would. I have seen him several times."

"Praise to God!" the shepherd answered. "I had heard it might be true. Where can I find him? I want to see him too!"

"I cannot tell you. He comes and then he leaves us. He is not with us most of the time."

They sat together that long afternoon and each told the other what had happened since they had last met in the courtyard of Caiaphas, the high priest. Peter told of going to the tomb early Sunday morning after the crucifixion and finding it empty except for the grave clothes. He told how Jesus had come to them while they were in a locked room still in great fear of their lives. There he showed them his hands that had been pierced by Roman spikes and his side that had received the thrust of the soldier's spear. He spoke of how Thomas, one of the twelve disciples, who was not with them in that room, would not believe it was really Jesus. But eight days later, when they were all together again, Jesus had suddenly appeared. Thomas was asked to touch the hands and side of Jesus. It was then that he exclaimed, "My Lord and my God!"

The shepherd told Peter of watching Jesus die on the cross and of the thief who received Jesus' forgiveness and eternal life. He told of the suffering he witnessed, of the hate and sorrow that was present around the cross. And he told of carrying Jesus to the tomb and the rich important men who were with him.

They talked about these and many other things that afternoon as busy throngs of people went about their routines of life in that marketplace in Jerusalem, the holy city of God. They agreed that Peter would ask Jesus when the shepherd could see him and he would then bring word for him when the time was right.

As they were departing, Peter spoke to the shepherd. "I need to thank you for those words you kept calling out to me as I was running away the night of Jesus' arrest. They may have saved my life and my soul. Do you remember them? 'Peter, he will forgive you. He will forgive you.'" With tears swelling in his eyes, Peter added, "He did. Jesus did."

And so the shepherd walked back to his home that evening and waited impatiently. For nearly a month he waited, wondering if he would ever see Jesus on this earth again. Wondering why he was not being sent for. Yes, more than wondering. Worrying, actually. Impatient worrying was his life while he watched his sheep, and at night, always the stars, waiting for Jesus to call for him. He knew that someday he must deal with his impatience, but he knew it could not be this time. He was sure of that.

Finally, one midmorning, his impatience, or perhaps his faith, was rewarded. Coming over the crest of a small hill was Peter. As he came closer, the shepherd thought about this strange man with such varied passions of love and caring, fear, and uncertainty, loyal to the core one moment, with fearful denial the next, open with his feelings, both tender and violent, depending on the circumstances.

Yet he felt Jesus had a special place for Peter in his heart and in his plans. "To be honest," the shepherd said smiling to himself, "that gives me comfort. There must be hope for me as well."

"Good morning, Simon Peter," the shepherd called out. "Is it time?"

"Good morning to you my friend and, yes, it is! When can you leave?"

"As soon as you are refreshed and have eaten," the shepherd replied.

"Good. The Lord is waiting for us near Jerusalem."

In the early afternoon as they approached Jerusalem, the shepherd once again looked over the ancient City of David. It glistened as the bright sun played its light on gigantic walls and gates, on the Roman theater, and Herod's palace, on structures centuries old, going back to the time of King David himself.

But most of all, it was the beautiful temple his eyes rested on that day with such love and adoration. The temple of wonderful memories and experiences. The place he loved more than any place on earth. Down through the Kidron Valley they walked, past the tomb of King David's son, Absalom, past the magnificent eastern gate, where Jesus had triumphantly entered only a few weeks before, to the Mount of Olives, the place of prayer, the place of betrayal, through groves of beautiful olive trees, some centuries old, until they came to an open area among the trees.

There the shepherd saw him. He stopped for a moment and their eyes met. Each walked toward the other until they were only a pace apart. Then the shepherd dropped to his knees, and with head bowed, said to his savior, "I worship you, my Lord and my God."

"My dearest friend, your worship and love is received with great love in return. You have been a good and faithful friend." Then Jesus brought the shepherd to his feet and embraced him, and repeated again, "My good and faithful friend."

He paused and then said, "I wanted to see you one last time on this earth before I return to my Father in heaven."

The shepherd asked, "O' Lord, when will you leave us?"

"That is why you are here, my son. But before I leave, there are things I want to tell you." Jesus was silent for a moment and then spoke quietly to the shepherd. "During the rest of your life on this earth you will go through times of hardship and sorrow, but you will also experience much joy and happiness in your life. Continue to love your Heavenly Father with all your heart, soul, and mind. Love all people, even your enemies."

Jesus smiled at the shepherd and said, "Even the Romans."

The shepherd smiled back and nodded.

"Tell all those you can about the good news of salvation. Tell them about the kingdom of God. Tell them about heaven."

"I will, my Lord. I will," whispered the shepherd.

Then Jesus clasped the shoulder of the shepherd, turned and went back to his disciples. For a few moments he spoke to them.

Then walking to a place between his disciples and the shepherd, Jesus raised his arms toward the sky as if in prayer. Then to their amazement he began to rise into the sky. Higher and higher he went until he disappeared into a cloud. They stared, speechless, for a long while. Suddenly, two men in white robes were with them. They said, "Men of Galilee, why are you standing here staring at the sky? Jesus has gone to heaven, and some day, just as he went, he will return."

When the angels had left, the disciples and the shepherd walked toward the eastern gate of the Holy City. When they reached the road in the Kidron Valley that would take the shepherd to Bethlehem, they stopped and Peter led them in prayer. Then they departed, the shepherd to his home and the disciples into Jerusalem, each to their own destiny.

The shepherd had many thoughts and questions on his way home that late afternoon. What did God want him to do next? Did God have something special for him to do? There must be some very important reason he had been so involved in his Lord's life.

But then he remembered the words of Jesus. Love God. Love all people. Jesus had called him his good and faithful friend. Twice. Maybe he wanted him to do just that. Love God. Love others. Do good. Be faithful.

The thought came to him. If he, with God's help and strength would strive for these things, everything else God might want him to do would be revealed to him when the time was right. And with that simple, yet profound understanding of God, the shepherd had peace.

Ten days after Jesus ascended into heaven, the holy feast day of Pentecost (also called the Feast of Weeks and the Feast of Harvests) was celebrated in Jerusalem. Pentecost was the second of three holy feast days for the Jewish people, a time of thanksgiving for the crops they had harvested. Jews from all over the known world would gather for this holy festival.

On the day before Pentecost, nine days after he had left Peter and the others in the Kidron Valley, the shepherd returned to celebrate with them this holy day of thanksgiving. He also wanted to see how they were coping without the Lord being with them for the first time in nearly two-and-one-half years.

The shepherd would return often to Jerusalem in the years that followed. But the rest of his life would be bracketed by two of these visits, the first of which he was making this very day, as he trudged up the hillside from the Kidron Valley to the gate of the city.

By noon he had found them, the disciples and many other followers of Jesus, in a house not far from the temple. For the rest of the day and evening he participated in their activities of prayer, reading the Holy Scriptures, praising God, and enjoying the company of each other. In the evening, just before supper, they all took part in a ceremony of remembering Jesus.

Peter took some loaves of bread and began breaking them in pieces and serving them to everyone in the house. When everyone had received some bread, he led them in a prayer of thanksgiving for their savior. Then he said to them, "Jesus told us, 'This bread is my body given for you. Eat it in remembrance of me.'"

When they had finished eating the bread, Peter took some cups of wine and began passing them around the crowded house. As he served the wine, he said, "Jesus told us, 'This is my blood, poured out for many to seal this new agreement between God and man to forgive your sins. Drink it in remembrance of me.'"

When they were finished, they had an evening meal together and afterward sang some hymns before returning to their homes.

Long into the evening the shepherd and Peter and a few of the other followers talked about the teachings of Jesus and what might come to pass in their lives. They wondered together about the prophecy of the temple being destroyed. They pondered how and when the Holy Spirit would come to comfort and guide them. So many unknowns lay ahead of them. So many uncertainties to face. But the thread of truth that ran though each of their minds and hearts, was that God would always be faithful and he would never leave them.

They gathered at dawn the following morning, this group of Jesus believers, this church in the making. Several of the disciples led in prayer for God to bless their day. As John was about to finish his prayer there came a tremendous roaring sound in the sky above them. To the shepherd it sounded like the worst windstorm he had ever experienced while watching his flocks around Bethlehem. Then the noise began to fill the house in which they were meeting. Suddenly, coming down on their heads, there appeared what seemed to be flames or tongues of fire.

The shepherd expected pain but felt none. Instead, into his mind, heart, and soul there came a mighty filling of what he, somehow, instantly recognized as the Holy Spirit. It was the most powerful feeling he had ever experienced in his life. And not only himself, but as he looked about the room, everyone present with him was experiencing the same thing.

As the wind subsided, another amazing sound was heard. All those in the room began speaking in languages they themselves could not understand. At the same time there were in Jerusalem devout Jews from many nations speaking numerous languages. When they and others who lived in the city heard the roaring wind above the house, huge crowds came running to see what was happening. When they began talking to those who came out from the house they were stunned to hear their native language being spoken to them by these followers of Jesus.

There were Jews and Jewish converts from a multitude of countries throughout the known world. As one of them said, "How can this be? For these men are from Galilee, and yet we hear them speaking all of the native languages of the lands where we were born! Parathians, Medes, Elamites, Mesopotamia, Judea, Cappadocia, Pontus, Asia Minor. Phrygia, Pamphylia, Egypt, Libya, Rome, Crete, Arabia. And we all hear these men telling in our own languages about the mighty power of God!"

Most who gathered were amazed and perplexed, not understanding the meaning of what they were witnessing. But others had an easy answer. "They're drunk," they mocked, "that's all!"

The shepherd saw Peter step forward and hold up his arms for the crowd to be silent. Over their murmurs, Peter began talking to them. He refuted that any were drunk. The prophet Joel had predicted what was happening centuries ago.

"In the last days," God said, "I will pour out my Holy
Spirit upon all mankind,
And our sons and daughters shall prophesy,
And your young men shall see visions,
And your old men dream dreams.
Yes, the Holy Spirit shall come upon all my servants,
men and women alike,
And they shall prophesy.
And I will cause strange demonstrations in the heavens
and on the earth,
Blood and fire and clouds of smoke . . ."

Peter talked to them of Jesus' death and resurrection. He told them of Jesus' promise to send the Holy Spirit and what they had witnessed that day was the Spirit coming in full power into their lives. Many who came and heard were moved deeply by these words. They asked Peter and the other apostles what they should do.

Peter replied, "Each one of you must turn from sin, return to God, and be baptized in the name of Jesus Christ for the forgiveness of your sins. Then you shall also receive this gift, the Holy Spirit. For Christ has promised him to each one of you who has been called by the Lord our God, and to your children and even to those in distant lands!"

Then Peter preached a long sermon, telling them about Jesus and urging them all to repent and be saved. The shepherd was awestruck by the response of the huge crowd. About three thousand men, women, and children who heard the message preached by Peter believed and were baptized. These same people, many from faraway lands returned to their own countries after Pentecost, and the message of Jesus Christ began to spread throughout the world.

Those who lived in Jerusalem began to meet regularly in small groups in each other's homes for teaching, prayer, and communion services in remembrance of Jesus. But for worship they would all meet together at the beautiful temple of God.

Each day brought to this group of believers new people who were coming to know about Jesus and believe in him. And the people of Jerusalem were accepting what was happening in their city. They were responding positively to the preaching of God's word, the people's zeal for worship, and the wonderful brotherly love that was felt by all who came in touch with the lives of the believers of Jesus.

And so from these believers the church began, the church of Jesus Christ.

Groups of believers, some large, some small, gathered first in Jerusalem, then spread throughout Judea and the other provinces of Israel, and into other countries as the gospel of Jesus Christ was carried throughout the world. The church grew as the Holy Spirit worked in the lives of the followers of Jesus who preached, taught, and lived the message of the good news of their Messiah.

The shepherd was part of this growing church. Through his witness and the witness of others, a group of believers began meeting in Bethlehem. The people in Israel were responding favorably to this new addition to their Jewish faith. To those who believed, Judaism was not being forsaken, but rather made complete in their Messiah, Jesus.

But there was one group who did not respond well to the "new religion." The Jewish leadership, the ruling religious body of the Jews, known as the Sanhedrin, began to fear this explosion of Jesus followers. So they began a persecution that would follow the church for centuries all over the world.

But even with this persecution the church grew and spread, as believers told of the wonderful way of salvation in Jesus, the way to God and his heavenly home.

The years passed and the shepherd grew old. By the time he reached the age of eighty-one, by his careful count, he was grandfather to sixty-three grandchildren, seventy-five great-grandchildren, and five great-great-grandchildren. Yes, he was the patriarch of his extensive family and very proud of it.

He and his wife still lived in the same house outside of Bethlehem, where he had raised his family, and where he still managed his flocks, though much smaller then in earlier years. All his sons and daughters were still living and none lived more than a few hours away.

The church in Bethlehem had grown in numbers and maturity since its beginning after that Holy Spirit Pentecost Day thirty-five years ago. Through these years the shepherd had become a powerful preacher, proclaiming the good news of salvation and helping lead his church toward spiritual maturity.

The persecution of the "new religion" increased steadily after the church was born at Pentecost. But it seemed the more the persecution, the stronger and more viable the followers of Jesus became. The years since the church had begun thirty-five years before had been good in many ways. The church had thrived and matured, but at a price, always a price. Many believers, who were now often called Christians, had been put in prison or killed for the cause of Christ.

Stephen had been the first to die in 35 A.D. But Paul, one of those who killed him, became a believer soon afterwards, spreading the message of Jesus throughout the known world, especially to the Gentiles. In the years that followed, the shepherd would hear of nearly all the apostles of Jesus dying a martyr's death for the cause of their savior. The exception would be his close friend, John, who would be exiled on the Island of Patmos for the rest of his life.

Over the years the shepherd would describe in great detail, to all who would ask about it, and to some who would not, the life of Jesus as he had observed it, particularly the events centering around his birth and his death on the cross.

He talked to all the Gospel writers at one time or another. Matthew, one of the disciples, had heard the stories many times. Luke, the doctor and associate of Paul, had faithfully recorded his words. Mark, a missionary with Paul and Barnabas, had listened to him. And of course, his dear friend, John, who would write the fourth gospel, three letters, and the great Book of Revelation, had often heard the wonderful stories he loved to tell.

In one of his early sermons the shepherd had embellished slightly one of the events in the life of Jesus. His eldest son had questioned him about it, and, with great humiliation, he clarified it in his next sermon. He had learned a lesson he would never forget.

In early winter of 65 A.D. great sorrow came to the shepherd's life. His wife of fifty-nine years suddenly became ill. For five days the shepherd, his family, and the church prayed for her life to be spared. But she herself told them she was ready to meet Jesus, and since she had never met him on earth, heaven would be the perfect place. Her only request was that she be buried on the Mount of Olives overlooking the holy temple. Within two days of her request, they buried her there. The shepherd, after the burial, asked that he be buried next to her upon his own death.

But what was beginning to take place in the land of Israel that year would prevent his family from ever honoring this desire of their father.

For in the year 65 A.D., a combination of events, both natural and man-made, caused great unrest among the Jewish people. Near famine conditions had existed for some time, resulting in terribly poor crops. In addition to the hunger and misery, there was the heavy Roman tax to which the Jews were forcibly subjected. The Roman-appointed ruler, Agrippa II, a Jew who was always loyal to Rome, had continuing conflicts with the Jewish religious leaders. He dismissed the high priest. Riots broke out in Jerusalem.

By this time the Jewish community had a full range of attitudes toward their Roman rulers, from open collaboration with the authorities to a call for armed resistance by the zealots. In the middle was the majority of the people, offering sullen but passive resistance. But even this group was beginning to move toward rioting and more active confrontation with the hated Romans. Rebellion was becoming open and more deadly.

The Romans had no intention of allowing this Jewish rebellion to continue and spread further. And so for the next four years Roman armies were sent into Israel to wipe out this deficiency within the Roman Empire, to destroy once and for all these Jews who were so obstinate and stubborn.

The Romans came and conquered region by region, until by 68 A.D. most of Israel had been retaken except for Jerusalem and a few other strong points of resistance. Due to political changes in Rome, the emperor Nero had been assassinated, there was a lull in Roman fighting until the early part of the fateful year of 70 A.D.

In the early spring of that year Jerusalem prepared to meet the delayed Roman assault. It was launched by the Roman general, Titus, on May 8, 70 A.D. Throughout the summer months, the assault on the city continued, with eighty thousand Roman troops battling twenty-five thousand Jewish fighters. On May 25 the first wall of the city was breached using battering rams and giant slings that could hurl rocks up to five hundred yards into the city.

Hand-to-hand fighting slowed the Roman advance, but advance they did, slowly but steadily toward the holy temple of God.

The years since his wife had died had been difficult for the shepherd. Three of his grandsons had been killed fighting the Romans. He now lived alone, but nearby was a large number of his family. He could see them every day and for that he was thankful. But he missed his wife very much and that was hard, very hard.

Yet his love and trust in God had not wavered and always part of his daily prayer was praise to his Lord for all he had received and experienced in life, and for God's will to be done with the holy temple he loved so much.

In late August, as the hot Middle East sun beat down on his house in the early afternoon, the shepherd became very tired and laid down on his bed to rest. As he slept, he dreamed. He dreamed he was on a hill, and from his hill he could see a lavish panoramic view of the golden city of Jerusalem. And on its eastern edge, glimmering in the dazzling sunlight, was God's beautiful holy temple.

In his dream, the Temple Mount seemed to glow and move as if dancing in the brilliance of the sun's rays. For seemingly a long while he drank in this spectacular vision with great pleasure and immense love.

But then the vision began to change. Gradually the city seemed to become twisted and mangled and dark. And where the Temple Mount had existed earlier in his dream there was now nothing but a darkened area of blackened debris.

He awoke, drenched in sweat and shaking. A dream as powerful as this had to be of immense importance with great meaning. This he knew. Of this he was certain. And with that certainty came the realization he was to go see his temple. Or at least try. Even if it meant death, he must try.

Late in the evening of August 27, 70 A.D., after he knew most were asleep, the shepherd packed some food and water and quietly slipped out of Bethlehem to head north toward Jerusalem. He would have to travel across country. It would not do to have a chance meeting with Roman soldiers on the road this night. At a time such as this, they would want more from him than toting luggage for a mile.

It was a very hard journey for the shepherd, these ten miles that seemed like one hundred. He was eighty-six years old, he told himself. Now that was hard to believe. Soon he would be an old man, he thought with a smile.

He had prayed before he left home for safety on his journey to Jerusalem, although he was really not worried about getting there safely. Why would God want him to go if he were not going to get him there safely? The return trip, however, was a different matter altogether!

Instead of the usual three or four hours, it took the shepherd seven hours to walk the ten miles from Bethlehem to a small hill, similar to the one in his dream, east of Jerusalem's east gate. The last mile and a half was the hardest for the shepherd, as he skirted around the quiet, sleepy outposts of Roman sentries.

Finally, before dawn he settled into a small hollowed cave that was hidden from view, but still would give him a good sighting of the city when daylight broke. In the distance he could see small fires burning throughout much of the city and around the Temple Mount. But where the temple was, there were no fires. He was thankful.

Dawn came and the shepherd could see huge battering rams next to the wall of the Temple Mount and thousands of soldiers milling around. They began to batter a portion of the wall and soon it was breached. Hundreds of soldiers poured in the opening. Fires were being set. Smoke poured into the sky and partially blocked the shepherd's view. The fighting continued for several hours. Finally, the shepherd saw flames coming from the temple itself. Over the next three to four hours they grew and grew until the entire Temple Mount appeared as an inferno of flames.

Josephus, a Jewish leader, witnessed the battle. In his own words he wrote, "The flames of fire were so violent and impetuous that the mountain on which the temple stood resembled one large body of fire, even from its foundation."

Throughout the afternoon the shepherd watched the terrible scene. His temple was being destroyed before his very eyes. Why did this have to be? Why destroy something so beautiful and sacred? With great sadness he watched as the fire burned and destroyed the most wonderful place on earth. Tears did come to his eyes, of course, but many times during that day of sorrows he remembered how very few things were permanent in his life. Only his relationship with his Lord would last beyond the grave. Jesus had said the temple would be destroyed, and now it had happened. But he still sorrowed. Such great sorrow.

By the time it was dark, the fire that had consumed the temple had lessened. The shepherd knew it was time to leave and he also knew it would be the last time he would ever be here. With the fall of Jerusalem, the danger to all Jews in the area would be immense. With great difficulty he headed for Bethlehem many hours away.

By the time he reached his home at dawn, the news of the temple's destruction and the fall of Jerusalem had reached Bethlehem. People were streaming south and away from the center of the Roman forces. A grandson he especially loved and to whom he was close saw him in the confusion of the escaping refugees.

"Grandfather," he shouted, "Where have you been? We must leave this place!"

The shepherd told him where he had been and what he had seen and his grandson was shaken by the story he told.

And so they left Bethlehem, the City of David, his home of eighty-six years, he and his grandson and a few others, and started the journey to the place called Masada.

It took them four days of struggle in the fiery August sun to reach their place of safety, this plateau on a mountain refuge. The climb to the summit nearly finished the shepherd. But after a terrible struggle he finally reached the top, and what he saw on the mountain amazed him.

It had been over a hundred years since King Herod had built the numerous structures on Masada. They included magnificent palaces, a swimming pool, a bathhouse, and, of course, the elaborate fortifications that protected the mountain fortress. The casement wall built around the circumference of the plateau was 4,250-feet long. Masada was shaped like a very wide boat. Its length was 1,900 feet from north to south, and its width, 650 feet from east to west.

It was an unbelievable place, the shepherd thought. And with that thought he slept for nearly a full day, his exhaustion was so great.

For the next three years the community of Jews at Masada lived in relative comfort, but under continual stress, as the Romans brought their mighty power against them. They were the remaining Jewish resistance in Israel, and they had to be crushed at all costs. There were less than a thousand of them on that mountaintop, including women and children. They were more symbolic than anything else, but a thorn in the side of Roman pride, nevertheless. The full weight of Roman power came against them in 72 A.D. in the form of the Roman Tenth Legion and thousands of slaves. A siege wall was built around the entire mountain to prevent escape by the Masada Jews, an amazing undertaking for such a seemingly small prize.

Then came construction of a ramp, even more astounding, on which the Romans would launch their attack. It started at the base of the mountain and reached nearly to the summit. Dirt and stones were piled against the mountain until the ramp was 400 feet high and 645 feet in length.

When the ramp was completed, a high wooden siege tower nearly ninety feet high was constructed at its top. From this tower grapefruit size stones were catapulted into Masada, causing havoc and destruction. Life was becoming more and more difficult for the Jews at Masada.

It had been terribly hot that spring day of 73 A.D. The sun had beat down with great fury on Masada, as the shepherd lay exhausted on a mat in the last home of his life. Even in the shade of the stone structure he suffered. Finally and mercifully, he fell into a fitful and wet sleep.

His grandson woke him at suppertime. As the family ate, there was silence around the table and great sadness. The end was near. They all knew. After they had eaten, the shepherd walked slowly around the huge fortress. He had felt a little stronger since his rest. He noticed the children were not playing as they usually did before sunset, before they were put to bed. He wondered what their fathers were saying to them, on what could be the last night of their lives.

In the distance he heard the noises of the Romans as they settled in for the night, thinking of the possible battle that could be fought the following day. From the edge of Masada he saw their fires, saw forms move, saw lives of men like himself, ready to kill, kill him and all those he loved at Masada.

What were they thinking? Was there hate for all the hardships these few Jews on Masada had put them through the past three years? He knew there was hate. There had to be hate. And fear. Fear of the coming battle that would kill and maim many of them. Fear of dying, of being no more. To cease existing when once you lived is a terrible thought. To die for what? To kill a few Jews, to capture a mountaintop? What was the point?

But the shepherd knew they had no choice, as well as they did. The soldiers would obey orders and fight and suffer and die for a cause that was, well, the cause of someone else, not theirs. It had happened that way for centuries and would happen for centuries in the future, wars owned by some men and fought by others.

He wondered how many Roman soldiers knew about Jesus and had believed in him. Probably some, he thought. Yes, some of the soldiers were believers in Jesus, he was sure. The truth of Jesus Christ had spread all over the known world by 73 A.D. The church had grown and thrived. Persecution made Christians flee Jerusalem and Israel like seeds in the wind, but fleeing did not weaken their love for Jesus and the story of that love they always told.

Thousands of Jews had been taken to Rome, fed to the lions, and made slaves to the Romans, but the Jewish faith lived on as did the Christian church, as they scattered out from Israel to the world beyond.

The following day the Romans, using battering rams mounted within the huge tower, knocked down a portion of the wall. To the surprise of the Romans, the Jews were able to rapidly rebuild the wall with wooden rams before an attack could be mounted. When the Romans set fire to the rams an unusual north wind began to blow and threatened to spread the flames on to the tower and destroy it. But then the wind shifted to the south and the wooden rams began to burn instead.

It was then the Jews knew they were doomed, probably within the day.

The historian, Josephus, gives an account of the speech that Eleazar, the leader of Masada, gave to the most courageous of his men after the flames destroyed their last defense. This is a portion of that speech.

> We were the very first that revolted from them,
> And we are the last to fight against them;
> And I cannot but esteem it as a favour that God hath
> granted us,
> That it is still in our power to die bravely,
> And in a state of freedom . . .
> It is very plain that we shall be taken within a day's time;
> But it is still an eligible thing to die after a glorious manner,
> Together with our dearest friends.

Let our wives die before they are abused,
And our children before they have tasted slavery;
And after we have slain them,
Let us bestow that glorious benefit upon one another mutually,
And preserve ourselves in freedom,
As an excellent funeral monument for us.

And so they died, all of them, except for two women and five children who hid themselves and lived to tell the story to the Romans and perhaps to the historian, Josephus. The last Jewish community in Israel had been destroyed.

This act of mass killings by the Masada leadership, although seemingly a brave and courageous act, has to be seriously questioned for both its spiritual and moral failures. Suicide certainly was never valued within the Jewish tradition. It is not a God-given option for his people. An assumption can be made that many of the approximately one thousand men, women, and children on Masada did not want to die of suicide. Seven women and children had to hide themselves to avoid being killed by the Masada leadership. For those who did die in this unwilling way, their deaths have to be considered acts of murder, not heroic deaths. These deaths at Masada on that hot spring day are an example of men wanting to control their own destiny, rather than desiring for God to be in control. In this dramatic event, the spiritual and moral wisdom of the Masada leadership was severely lacking.

On the previous evening, after the shepherd had walked around the edge of Masada, he went to his mat and as he laid down to sleep, thinking that perhaps he would die the next day. And with that thought he knew what he wanted to do. He gathered up his bedroll and walked to the center of Masada and laid his mat on the ground. He would sleep there tonight under the stars, under his stars.

Strange, he thought, how they had not changed since he was a boy. All in there places, the animals, the people, the big and little dippers. All there. As he gazed into the brilliant starlit sky he remembered so long ago when he was young, a little shepherd boy, who was visited by angels and told about a baby who was the Messiah, the savior of the world, his Lord.

He remembered it as if it were yesterday, running into Bethlehem that winter night and finding the baby Jesus lying in a manger just as the angel had said. He remembered the star that had led the rich men from eastern lands to Bethlehem to worship Jesus, and then how he, too, had first worshiped his Lord.

He also remembered the cruel killings of the children and his hatred that grew for the Romans. But that hatred was no more, even at a time like this, when Roman soldiers were about to kill them all. He had found Jesus and his forgiveness, and Jesus had told him not to hate but to love. He now knew that worked best. Even tonight it worked best.

He thought of that horrible day Jesus died on the cross, and the suffering he went through for him, so that he might be in heaven with Jesus someday.

And then he prayed. He thanked God for his life, for his family, for Jesus, and the salvation he had received because of him. He finished his prayer by praying aloud, "Dear Lord, would this not be a good time to take me into your heaven? I am ready. It was hard to love the Romans, but I do love them because you love me so much. I don't want to be killed by someone I love."

When he had finished praying a quiet peace came over the shepherd and he went to sleep. As he slept he dreamed of stars, brilliant, shining stars, beaming down on his flocks as he shepherded them through the night.

Then in his dream he saw a star that began to grow larger and larger and seemingly come toward him. As it came closer, the light became brighter than even the sun until it had encompassed his very being.

He began to hear singing like that of the angels so long ago. They were singing praises to God and to Jesus, the Lamb of God.

The shepherd began to walk through the light until in the distance he saw someone walking toward him. As they came closer together he knew it was Jesus. He began running and when they met he fell at the feet of his Lord, and prayed, "I worship you, Jesus, my Lord and my God."

Jesus smiled and brought him to his feet and said, "Welcome home, my good and faithful friend."

Then Jesus held the shepherd boy in his arms.

# PART 3

## THE WAYS OF GOD

# THE WAY

*Before anything else existed*
*There was Christ, with God.*
*He has always been alive and is himself God.*
*He created everything there is.*
*Nothing exists that he did not make.*
*Eternal life is in him,*
*And his life gives light to all mankind.*

*In the beginning God created the heavens and the earth,*
*Light and Darkness,*
*Water and Sky,*
*Earth,*
*Vegetation,*
*Sun and Moon,*
*Fish,*
*Birds,*

*Animals of the earth,*
*And then he created you and me.*
*Oh, of course, he created Adam and Eve first.*
*But he was certainly thinking of us!*
*God made us in his own image,*
*To be blessed by God and given rule*
*Over the earth for his glory.*
*God saw what he did was good and then he rested.*

*The Eden we were to live in was a perfect place.*
*God wanted it that way because he loved us so much.*
*There were to be no evil or bad things in the world.*
*Death*
*Sickness*
*Loneliness*
*Crying*
*Pain*
*Hopelessness*
*Sadness*
*Rejection*

*There were only good things.*
*Joy*
*Fulfillment*
*Honesty*
*Love*
*Contentment*
*Peace*
*And an immense number of other*
*Wonderful human needs and desires.*

*God asked one thing of us as*
*Human beings whom he created.*
*Obedience*

*But Adam and Eve did not obey God.*
*Nor have we down through the centuries of time.*
*No human being has been exempt.*
*All the way from Adam to you and me.*
*This disobedience is called sin.*
*It is sin that separates us from God.*
*It is sin that keeps us from eternity in heaven.*

*The great question that should be considered by everyone is*
*Who is going to heaven?*

*We know our body will someday die*
*And in time turn to dust.*
*The earthly body is temporary.*
*Our soul is permanent and eternal.*
*We live on through our soul in a new resurrected body*
*But where will we live after our lives are finished on earth?*

*God from the beginning created us to live with him.*
*To love him.*
*To worship him.*
*To exist forever in his presence.*
*Who did he choose for his heaven?*
*He chose everyone!*

*And why would he do that for us?*
*Because*

*God so loved the world.*
*From Adam to the last person ever born.*
*He desired us from the beginning of time*
*To come into his heaven.*
*To live with him for eternity.*

*And God,*
*Who is God?*
*In the beginning was God.*
*In the beginning God created.*
*God has always been and always will be.*
*God is eternal.*
*God*
*Never changes*
*Is everywhere*
*Knows all things*
*Is all powerful*
*Is the only true God*
*Is just*
*Is holy*
*Loves*
*You and me.*

*Yet we sin.*
*We disobey God.*
*From God's Word, the Bible, we find,*
*"For all have sinned and come up short*
*Of what God wants for his glory."*
*"There is none that is good enough. Not one single person."*

*No good people on this earth for heaven?*
*Surely there is!*
*Mother Teresa?*
*Hitler? Probably not.*
*Does God draw a line somewhere between these two lives?*
*One side of the line makes it .*
*The other side loses out.*
*How good would we have to be?*
*How bad could we be?*
*And still make it to heaven.*
*You*
*Me*
*Where is that line? Am I there yet? Am I good enough?*
*Am I?*
*Am I?*

*The good news is that there is no line.*
*Nor could there be.*

*Why?*
*Because God is holy.*
*Sin cannot exist in God's heaven, in God's holy presence.*
*Even the smallest sin,*
*The smallest sin ever committed*
*Cannot be brought into heaven*
*By you*
*By me*

*When we die.*
*We must be perfect even as God is perfect,*

*But yet we all sin as we live on this earth.*
*And even though God wants every human being*
*Who ever existed*
*To live forever in his heaven,*
*That even from the beginning of time*
*God desired us for eternal life with him,*
*It is this sin in our life that will keep us from God's heaven*
*When we die.*

*If our soul cannot be in heaven to live*
*Where will we live?*
*Out of God's presence.*
*Out of God's heaven.*
*In hell.*

*What is hell?*
*A place*
*Not a "state of mind"*
*Satan is there*
*His demons*
*God is not there*
*Hopelessness*
*Pain*
*Darkness*
*Gnashing of teeth*
*Weeping*
*God is not there*
*Confusion*
*Terror*
*God is not there*
*No partying with friends*

*No friends*
*Loneliness*
*Regret*
*No jokes*
*God is not there*
*Solitary*
*Alone*
*Eternal*
*Forever*
*God is not there*
*Forever*
*Forever*
*Forever*

*God does not send people to hell.*
*People go to hell because there is no other place to go,*
*Except heaven.*

*What is heaven?*
*A place*
*God is there*
*Jesus is there*
*Joy*
*Peace*
*Happiness*
*Love*
*An eternal place*
*God is there*
*No tears*
*No hate*
*No fear*

*Contentment*
*Not boring*
*Exciting*
*Fulfillment*
*Worship*
*God is there*
*Reunion*
*Security*
*A beautiful place*
*A place of belonging*
*The most wonderful place ever conceived*
*God is there*
*Forever*
*Forever*
*Forever*

*Heaven is a place God has made for you and me.*
*But in heaven there can be no sin,*
*No people of sin*
*Like you and me.*

*How then can we go to heaven when we die?*
*There is only one way.*
*When our sins are removed from our souls*
*And not counted any more by God.*
*Without our sins God looks upon us as*
*Holy*
*Pure*
*Righteous*
*Sinless*
*A son or daughter*

*Acceptable to live in heaven*
*The way he always wanted us.*

*How does God go about doing this?*
*Removing our sins,*
*Your sins and mine.*
*He tells us in his Word the Bible.*
*Since you and I are guilty of sin,*
*Deserving of death,*
*Deserving of hell,*
*The cost of our sin must be paid.*
*God cannot just overlook our sin.*
*Remember,*
*He is a just and holy God.*
*But he loves us so much*
*That he in the beginning of time chose to pay*
*The terrible cost of our sin himself.*

*How?*
*By sending his son Jesus to earth to die for our sins*
*So we would not have*
*To die,*
*Go to hell,*
*Stay out of heaven.*

*And Jesus,*
*Who is Jesus?*
*He is the Christ,*
*God's son,*
*Part of the Trinity: Father, Son, Holy Spirit.*
*Present at creation*

*He is God*
*Our Savior*
*Our Redeemer*
*The Jew's Messiah*
*Conceived by the Holy Spirit*
*Born to a virgin woman*
*A human man for thirty five years*
*Hungered*
*Thirsted*
*Sinless*
*He is God*
*Love*
*Strong*
*Compassionate*
*Died for our sins*
*Rose from the dead*
*Returned to heaven*
*Lives*
*Forever*
*Forever*
*Forever*

*Jesus came to live on earth as a man.*
*Exposed to sin but was sinless.*
*Was tempted but resisted evil.*
*Lived the perfect life,*
*Yet had the passions of a man.*
*He came for one reason.*
*To die,*
*To bleed,*
*To be broken.*

To fulfill God's requirement that our sins,
Yours and mine
Be taken away.

It happened on a
Cross,
A Roman cross,
At Jerusalem, Israel,
Two thousand years ago.
When Jesus, God in human flesh, hung, bled
And died on that cross
He took our sins on himself
To pay the penalty for our sins
So we can go to heaven
When we die.

Jesus died on a Friday.
On the third day, Sunday,
He rose from the dead
Out of the sealed tomb his followers had placed him.
Christ Jesus had risen
From death to life
For eternity,
Forever!

For forty days he stayed on earth.
Seen by hundreds.
Teaching many of his followers.
Walking among them
Until the day he returned to heaven.
His disciples saw him

*Rise into the sky.*
*Leave them.*

*Even though they were full of joy*
*They had to be sad.*
*He was gone.*
*Gone from their lives they thought,*
*Perhaps forever.*
*But yet they knew he had told them*
*He would send a comforter,*
*The Holy Spirit,*
*To give them guidance, strength, and comfort.*

*And the Holy Spirit,*
*Who is the Holy Spirit?*
*Part of the Trinity of God: Father, Son, Holy Spirit*
*Present at creation*
*Eternal*
*Holy*
*Our comforter*
*Convincer of sin*
*A guide for our lives*
*Inspirer*
*Revealer of truth*
*A direction giver*
*Convincer of sin*
*A regenerator of lives*
*An assurer*
*Teacher*
*An indweller in our lives*

*Convincer of sin*
*Yet a comforter*

*The Holy Spirit*
*Shows human beings their sinfulness,*
*Convicts us that we are sinful,*
*Unworthy of living with God in his heaven.*
*But the Holy Spirit does not stop there.*
*He can show us not only our need for God,*
*But how we can know God.*
*And have the assurance we will go to heaven*
*When we die.*

*If we let him.*
*If we want to let him.*

*How then do we come into the family of God for eternity?*
*We come through faith.*
*Believing through faith in what God did*
*To bring you and I into his family,*
*Into his heaven.*

*Faith,*
*The faith to believe that only through Christ's death*
*On the cross for our sins*
*Can God take away our sins from our soul.*

*Faith*
*Faith to believe there is no other way to come to God*
*Except to believe in this plan of God.*

But more than just believing intellectually
That there is but one God,
That Christ is God's son,
That Christ died for our sins,
There must come a time in one's life,
Yours and mine,
In one way, one form or another,
When we cry out to God
That
I am a sinner.
I cannot save myself.
I need his forgiveness.
I am without hope for eternity.
I am unworthy of approaching the one true and living God.
Yet I do.
And
I ask God for his mercy.
I ask God for his salvation,
To save me
For his heaven
For eternity.

And because we know that Christ died for our sins
We ask Jesus Christ to be our savior.
We tell him of our desire to turn from our sin
And walk in his way
Toward him.

And how does God respond
To
Our crying out to him,

*Our asking him to forgive our sins,*
*Our believing in Christ as our savior?*
*He rejoices!*
*He forgives our sins and takes them away*
*From our soul forever.*
*He gives us eternal life from that moment on.*
*We receive a new life.*
*We are reborn into the kingdom of heaven.*
*And when we die we will live in heaven*
*And see God,*
*Forever,*
*Forever,*
*Forever!*

*Who is going to heaven?*
*You?*
*Me*

*May it be so.*

# Is God Fair?

There are many ways to describe God's character. We know about God from reading the Holy Scriptures. We can experience God as we live our lives here in his world.

God shows his love toward us in many ways. He is patient and long-suffering when we disobey him. He is a giving, caring, generous God who always wants the best for his people he created.

We also know that he is a holy God and he cannot tolerate sin in his heaven, but because he loves us so much he provided a way of escape from our sin.

There are some questions, however, we may want to think about.

Can every person who ever lived, and every person who ever will live, escape from their sin and go to heaven if they choose to? Or does God pick and choose who may come into his heaven? And would that be fair if he did? Could

God be unfair if he wanted to be? Certainly, he is God. But is it in the character of God to be unfair? Is it within God's nature to be unfair? Not at all!

To answer the question, is God always fair? The answer has to be a resounding, yes! Therefore, every person who ever lived, and every person who ever will live, can escape from their sin through God's plan and live eternally in heaven if that is what they choose.

Another question to consider. Does God know who will be in his heaven and who will be out of his presence when they die? Yes, he knew this from the beginning of time. But although God knows this about us, he does not prevent our determining for ourselves our eternal destiny. It is our choice. God made his choice. He has chosen us. We will choose or reject his plan for us. In doing so we will choose or reject God.

And one more question. Would it be fair for God to keep all the people he created out of his heaven because of our sin? Yes, but God's grace prevented that from happening. Because he loved us so much he came in human form to die on a cross so our sins could be taken away and forgiven.

Jesus Christ, the savior of the world, the redeemer of mankind, whose death on the cross paid the penalty for the sins of the world, for everyone who ever lived and ever will live, his sacrifice is sufficient for God.

But think of all the people of the world who ever lived and ever will live, from the beginning of mankind until the last human who inhabits this earth. Billions of us, like the stars in the sky, from every nation, race, culture, religion, and political system, have existed over thousands of years, all of us created by God to live forever in his heaven.

Yet how many of these billions of people will have known of God's plan for receiving them into his heaven when they die? There are so many things to keep them from hearing about Christ's death on the cross for the redemption of their souls.

Some lived before the time of Christ. How could they hear?

Many lived in places where God's plan could never have reached them for centuries after Christ's death on the cross: the Amazon River basin, the American plains, Australia, the jungles and deserts of Africa, the islands of the Pacific, and thousands of other places on earth. How could they hear?

Even today in our age of instant communication, there are people living in remote areas all over the world who have never been exposed in any way to this plan God has for them. Tribes in South America and the African bush, villages in India and Tibet, never hearing the good news of Christ.

And throughout the world people of different cultures and religions know about Jesus Christ as a religious individual, but have never heard about God's plan for them in a meaningful way: Buddhists from China, Hindus from India, Moslems from Africa the Middle East and America, Protestants and Catholics in America and Europe who attend churches that never clearly teach the truth of God's plan for mankind, Jews from Israel, Europe and America, the nonreligious from every continent on earth, and so on.

Of all these billions of people who ever lived on earth, very few will hear of God's plan of salvation. Very few will have the chance to accept or reject God's plan. Is this fair?

Certainly all the people living today do not have an equal chance to hear about God's plan of bringing them into his heaven? People who are exposed to those who know God's plan of salvation surely have a greater chance to hear about it: parents who tell their children, ministers who tell their congregations, missionaries who spread God's word to people to whom they minister, all who share this plan with their friends and loved ones.

People who are able to read God's word, the Bible, may understand God's salvation plan for them. Those who do not have access to God's word are deprived of this great resource God gave to mankind.

Is it fair that those who have never heard of God's plan for eternal life be denied a place in heaven? No, that certainly would not be fair.

Yet we know our God is fair. Since there are people who have lived in the past, live now in the present, or will live in the future, who will not hear about God's plan to bring them into his heaven by someone telling them, or having access to God's word, the Bible, what way has God, who loves them and is fair, provided for these people to come into his heaven?

The Bible tells us that since the creation of the world God's great and wonderful qualities are revealed. All mankind can see his power and divine nature through his created world. The complex creation of our natural world can reveal God to every man and woman who ever lived or ever will live.

We can see God in many ways through the world he created for us. The interdependence of animal life; the immense variety of vegetation; the complexity of minerals and earth materials; the universe with its systems of galaxies; the solar system and our own earth; our bodies, minds, and spirits making up our whole being; all of these function together in a way only a creator could design.

But is recognizing that a single God created the world enough to bring a person into a relationship with that God? The answer we find in God's word, the Bible has to be no, for even Satan believes there is a single God. He knows very well who is the true God of the universe. But he chose to break his relationship with God long ago. A very bad choice!

Part I, "Those Who Find Him," illustrated how God solved the problem when a man or woman never has the opportunity to hear the wonderful plan our Heavenly Father has for each of us. The stories of the lives of those men and women who answered the Holy Spirit's call on their lives can represent all humanity, any of us who ever lived or ever will live on this temporary home we call Earth.

Yes,
God is fair to all people.
All of us.

# CHOICES

But who are we really, you and I, created in God's image? How did he make us? What are we really like? How tightly did God tie us to himself? How closely are we connected to God's control?

In reality there is a paradox in the relationship between God and you and me. God holds us close to himself in his great and wonderful love and mercy. We are his people, the crowning jewel of his creation. He desires us to love and obey him, to center our lives on him, to worship and adore him, to be his people, totally and completely, forever.

Yet God has made us free men and women. We are not robots. He has given us a mind and spirit that are free, free to make choices, right choices, and wrong choices. We are free to go in any direction we desire, the right way, the wrong way.

Why did God give us this choice? Why does he not force us to obey him? He could. He is God. He is all-powerful. But if he left us with no choice but his choice, if we were just robots doing what he desired with no choice of whether to sin or not to sin, how then could we honor God through our obedience. How could we show our love to him if we had no choice but to obey?

We would be like the rocks and trees and oceans, existing but with no free will to follow and obey God. We would be slaves and not free men and women who are free to obey God because that is our desire, because we love him, want to serve him, and be in his heaven for eternity.

There will come a time in each of our lives when the Holy Spirit calls to us for the first time, through a relative or friend, as we read the Bible, listen to a sermon, or through the way a friend lives his life. Perhaps even as we observe the beauty and wonder of God's natural world, the Holy Spirit can enter our thoughts and mind to speak to us.

What is so great is that he leaves no one out, not you or me or anyone who ever existed. Every person he ever created is important to God, important to his kingdom. He calls everyone. He calls you. He calls me.

And when the Holy Spirit calls to us for the first time to begin to move toward God, it may be a small and simple step he urges us to take to begin our journey to heaven. Or it may be the call for us to cry out to him and confess our sin and claim Jesus Christ as our savior. Whatever the call, we must make our first choice.

The Bible tells us that many people will make the choice to reject the Holy Spirit's call for different reasons. They may believe God's plan is too simplistic. Many feel they need to work their way into heaven by being good enough, doing good things. Some may think they are too bad a person for God to want them. And some may think they are good enough to make it to heaven without any help. A few may question the reality of God. Is there a God? Is there a hereafter? Is there a hell? And the reasons go on and on, a reason for every rejection of God's call.

Does the Holy Spirit call to us only once and that's it? Does he give up the first time his call is rejected? Does he write us off? Done for. Let them go to hell!

No! God loves us so much, he wants us in his heaven so badly, he keeps on gently knocking at our hearts, for as long as we live.

But something happens when a person rejects the Holy Spirit's call that first time. A thin layer of hardness wraps around his mind, his heart, and his soul. And when the Holy Spirit calls him the second time, it is a little more difficult to hear, to feel his call.

With each succeeding rejection the layers of hardness build. The willingness, and even the ability to respond, to the call of the Holy Spirit begins to diminish in a person's life. The sound of his knocking becomes so faint, as he attempts to penetrate the layers of hardness, that it becomes almost easy to reject the Spirit's call.

Finally, perhaps, nothing is heard. Too many layers. Too many rejections.

In time, death comes and that person still has his sin in his soul. It has not been removed. The only sin unpardonable by God, the rejection of the Holy Spirit's call has occurred.

He cannot come into heaven. It is too late, too late.
The only place left to go is hell.
What a terrible mistake. What a terrible choice.

You?
May it never be so.

# Epilogue

## Eternity

Over the centuries and millennia of human existence there have lived on earth all the people of God's creation, each of whom have had a singular identity belonging only to them. Each of us has our own personality, our own developing character, and our own unique ability to respond to God's leading to come to him and eternal life in his heaven.

The ancient and not so ancient people described in this book also heard God's call, each one of them finding themselves on the stage of God's panoramic saga of human history. Are they real people? Did they really exist somewhere in time? In one sense, yes. The shepherd, the wall builder, the artist, the gang banger, and all the others represent the human race. They are each of us, with all our strengths and all our frailties.

As God so loves them, he also loves you and me.

As he gave to them the free choice to accept or reject him, so he gives to us this same free choice. When our life is over on this earth, our choice will have been made. Our destiny for eternity will be set forever.

King David of Israel once prayed this prayer to God.

> But as for me, my contentment is not in wealth but in seeing you
> And knowing all is well between us.
> And when I awake in heaven,
> I will be fully satisfied,
> For I will see you face to face.

> May we see God together in heaven someday,
> You and me.

> May it be so.

To order additional copies of

send $9.95 plus $3.95* shipping and handling to

WinePress Publishing
PO Box 428
Enumclaw, WA 98022

or have your credit card ready and call

(877) 421-READ (7323)

*add $1.00 for each additional book ordered